"How fast can you get your clothes off?" Alex asked with a grin

"In the car?"

"No—the race starts as soon as I unlock the front door. The first one who hits the bed stark-naked wins."

Olivia pretended to give the matter some thought. "What do I get if I win?"

He undid the buttons on her coat. "Anything you want," he murmured, slipping his hand under her sweater.

Olivia inhaled sharply as he moved his hand upward, his thumb pressing into the side of her breast with agonizing tenderness. His ability to turn her to jelly still surprised her. "And what if you win?"

He kissed her long and slow. "Next time we stay in the car."

Like Olivia Bennett in *All That Glitters*, **Kristine Rolofson** has little time for herself. Olivia has to juggle three children, a small business and a budding love affair—not very much different from Kristine's life! With six children and a marriage of twenty-two years, she rarely finds herself without company. Even as she types away at the computer her tiny dog, Charlie, sits faithfully at her feet. So why is it not surprising when Kristine admits, ''My secret vice is traveling''? Because when she travels, she goes *alone*.

Kristine's next book, #425 *The Perfect Husband,* launches Temptation's exciting and magical miniseries for 1993—Lovers & Legends. Imagine your favorite fairy tale retold Temptation-style! *The Perfect Husband* will be available in January 1993.

Books by Kristine Rolofson

HARLEQUIN TEMPTATION
179—ONE OF THE FAMILY
259—STUCK ON YOU
290—BOUND FOR BLISS
323—SOMEBODY'S HERO
348—THE LAST GREAT AFFAIR

Don't miss any of our special offers. Write to us at the following address for information on our newest releases.

Harlequin Reader Service
P.O. Box 1397, Buffalo, NY 14240
Canadian address: P.O. Box 603,
Fort Erie, Ont. L2A 5X3

ALL THAT GLITTERS

KRISTINE ROLOFSON

Harlequin Books

TORONTO • NEW YORK • LONDON
AMSTERDAM • PARIS • SYDNEY • HAMBURG
STOCKHOLM • ATHENS • TOKYO • MILAN
MADRID • WARSAW • BUDAPEST • AUCKLAND

With love to my oldest daughter, Nancy,
whose delight in creating earrings
inspired this story.
Special thanks also to Mark Morrison,
who patiently explained Ferraris to
a woman who drives an eight-year-old,
ten-passenger station wagon.

Published October 1992

ISBN 0-373-25515-2

ALL THAT GLITTERS

1

"CAN I HELP YOU with anything in particular?"

Alexander Leeds absentmindedly flashed his most devastating smile at the hovering saleswoman before returning to study the contents of the enormous display case. "Well, perhaps you can." He tapped the glass above a display of jewel-studded earrings. "Are these the Fancy Nancy collection?" He almost winced when he said it. *Fancy Nancy.* Was he actually thinking about representing a company with such a ridiculous name? It was better suited to gourmet popcorn. Or microwaved potato puffs.

The attractive silver-haired woman looked surprised. "Oh, no. The Fancy Nancys are hanging over there." She pointed to a spot past his right shoulder. "On the large rack on the counter by the window."

Alexander turned. Six strides and he was across the jewelry store, past a collection of beaded necklaces, a porcelain cat with bracelets hooked on its ears and a display of chunky necklaces. The saleswoman hurried over to pat the top of an earring stand. Dangling from its brass holder were the gaudiest earrings Alexander Leeds had ever set his beautiful brown eyes upon. Multicolored shapes of flowers and hearts were dusted with glitter and topped with beads and pearls. Plastic rhinestones decorated every available surface. "*These* are the Fancy Nancy earrings?"

"Oh, yes. And they're very popular, too," the woman assured him, adjusting the display with one long, manicured fingernail. "Especially around the holidays."

"I see." Alexander couldn't imagine any time of year when these particular earrings could be popular, but he exhibited his customary restraint and didn't say so. He lifted a pair of fuchsia hearts from the rack. The black card had Fancy Nancy scrawled in silver ink. When he turned it over, he saw that the price was an affordable $7.50. "Who buys these?"

"Young women, middle-aged women, teenagers."

"I see." He put down the purple pair and stared at the rest.

"The black ones go with practically anything," the saleswoman offered. "Especially the black ones with the little pearls in the center."

Alex obligingly hunted for the pearl earrings. Dusted with silver glitter, they looked like something a burlesque dancer would have glued to certain parts of her body. Seeing the humor, Alex decided to break his steadfast rule about buying jewelry for women and pulled his wallet from the inside pocket of his jacket.

"I'll take them," he said. He would add them to his secretary's bonus for her birthday. Paula always got a kick out of his odd gifts, although she hadn't been thrilled when he'd represented the new toilet-bowl-cleaner people. She'd informed him there was a limit to how many blue pellets one person could drop into a toilet tank before the excitement wore off.

The saleswoman stepped to the cash register and rang up the purchase, then tucked the earrings into a small brown bag. "Fancy Nancy is very popular because the price is reasonable and they're, well . . . *fun*."

"Fun," he echoed. He couldn't think of anything fun about earrings. Women loved them, though, and he loved women.

But he'd never met anyone wearing a pair of Fancy Nancys. He frowned, trying to remember if Olivia had been wearing glittery earrings when he'd introduced himself. He remembered the sophisticated black dress, the elegant topknot of blond hair, the deep blue eyes. Eyes that held warmth and intelligence. He'd noticed that right away. Well, he amended, remembering Olivia's legs, almost right away.

At four o'clock he was going to see Olivia Bennett again, the beautiful woman who needed his expertise to make her company a success. She and the other members of her jewelry company would spend this windy Saturday afternoon discussing how Alexander P. Leeds, hotshot marketing consultant, could turn Fancy Nancy into a household word and make everyone concerned a pile of money. That was his job and he was damn good at it. When he wanted to be. But right now he wasn't sure if he wanted to get into the earring business or not.

Alex thanked the woman and tucked the bag into his jacket pocket. Stepping outside into the frigid wind, he shivered, remembering the recent days spent blissfully alone on a beach in Aruba. He'd been crazy to return so soon, but work had piled up during his absence, and unfortunately for his romantic plans to see Olivia again, Fancy Nancy was one of the companies he'd had to stall. Alex looked at his Rolex. He had two hours and three more stores to visit before deciding if he and Fancy

Nancy had a future together. He already knew he and Olivia did.

"I CAN'T GO THROUGH another Christmas like this last one," Olivia said. "It would absolutely do me in."

"We made money." Her son's blond head tilted closer to the flashing green numbers on the computer screen.

Olivia thought of the piles of bills waiting to be paid. "Not enough."

She saw Josh grin. "Never enough."

"I have nightmares about glitter." Olivia walked to the dining room window to watch the naked trees bend with the wind. The sky was dreary, a furious shade of gray that made this January afternoon look particularly bleak and miserable. No snow softened the winter landscape of brown grass. "And glue," she added, shoving her hands inside her jeans pockets. "Sometimes I dream I've glued myself to the bed."

"Don't worry, Mom. We're all gonna be rich someday."

"Think so?"

"Yeah. The numbers don't lie." He grinned again. "And that guy is comin' today to tell us how to do it."

"I know." *Believe me, I know.* "That guy" was one of the best-looking men Olivia had ever met. Tall, dark and handsome, with a smile to make a woman beg for mercy. Even an ordinary woman like herself with an abundance of common sense. Of course, common sense had been the last thing she'd had on her mind at Judd's Christmas party where they'd met.

"We'll be ready for him."

"Good." *The question is, will I?*

"Whaddya want when we're rich, Mom?"

"I think I'll buy new furniture," Olivia said, picturing the faded couch in the living room. "And a new car," she added. "Maybe one of those minivans."

"When I get rich I'm gonna go on a cruise."

Olivia turned to stare at him. "A cruise? I didn't think thirteen-year-olds went on cruises."

"Yeah. It's cool. Brandon and his folks went on one after Christmas."

Brandon again. Brandon with the grandparents who owned three popular Rhode Island chicken restaurants. Olivia picked a pile of papers from a dining room chair and dumped them onto the floor. Then she sat down and stared at the computer screen. "Are we rich yet?"

"Not yet, Mom. The cash flow is a problem."

"Tell me about it."

"Nah," her son answered. "You wouldn't understand it, anyway."

"Is that a sexist remark?"

Josh peered at her over his gold-rimmed glasses. He looked like a very intelligent stockbroker, which was what he planned to be. "Mom, you know me better than that. But the last time I tried to explain everything you fell asleep."

"You're right." Just the thought of listening to Josh droning on about the numbers made her want to yawn. The bottom line was all that counted.

"And all that you want to know is the bottom line," he said.

"True." Olivia moved restlessly on the chair. She really needed to pick up this mess before the meeting, especially since she wanted to make a good impression. She'd had every intention of completely cleaning the house, really she had. But buying groceries came before vacuuming, and putting food away came before cleaning the bathroom. It was a matter of priorities. Olivia was good at prioritizing, even when Alexander Leeds would arrive in less than an hour. She fought the panicky urge to vacuum everything in sight. "But I should study all this. I think I should sound knowledgeable before Alex—Mr. Leeds arrives."

"You will," her son assured her. "I'm working up a business plan that everyone will understand."

"You're a good kid. Go out and play."

"Nah. I'd rather do this. Then I can finish my Stephen King book."

Olivia would have liked to go outside. If only there were snow! Playing in the snow seemed preferable to cleaning the house before the upcoming meeting. But this January there was no snow, just a cold wind from the Atlantic that would not stop blowing through the small seaside community. Sometimes when she walked from work to her car, her breath blew back into her lungs. A trip to Florida would be nice right now. Was that where Alex had gone on his vacation? She turned back to Josh, still hunched over the table. "Are you sure you're only thirteen?"

"Yeah," he agreed absently, his mind clearly on the numbers spread in front of him. "You were there."

"Don't be fresh." She spoke mildly. The children teased her all the time, but she gave back as good as she got. "Where's Wolf?"

"He'll be back in a minute. He went to put gas in the car."

"Nancy?"

"Downstairs. She's trying to finish her horse painting."

"The meeting's in an hour. Are we going to be ready?"

"Yeah, Mom, no problem."

Olivia knew that was what he'd say. Her sons took good care of her: Wolf handled the practical chores and Josh dealt with the finances. Still, it was up to her to make the decisions, although everyone in the family voiced an opinion on just about every topic. The bottom line was that she, Olivia Bennett, age thirty-six and counting, was responsible for making sure the family had everything it needed—emotionally and physically. She wasn't complaining, but damn—sometimes she felt so tired.

Olivia stepped away from the window and scooped a pile of clean clothes off the diningroom table. She had high hopes for today. She was reaching for the stars and fully expected to capture a handful.

ALEX DROVE ALONG Matunuck Beach Road and checked the numbers on the mailboxes that lined the narrow street to the ocean. He'd known Olivia's business was a home-based one, so the sight of the nondescript Cape Cod cottage with its weathered shingles came as no surprise when he drove up to the address he'd been given over the telephone. This was supposed to be a full-fledged, informal session about what he could do for Fancy Nancy, but Alex had his doubts.

He couldn't do much, he'd decided. The fashion business was as fickle as an eighth-grade girl, and Alexander wasn't going to waste his time putting together a program for something that would be out of style before it ever hit the stands. But he'd promised he would attend the meeting and it wasn't good business to break a promise. Besides, he planned to invite Olivia to dinner afterward. It was the dinner they should have had after Judd's party, but he'd been off to catch a plane. And she had mysteriously whispered of her plans to decorate a Christmas tree. The pang of jealousy still surprised him.

Alex stepped out of the car, avoiding the icy patches on the sidewalk, climbed two brick steps to the front door and rang the bell. His breath came out in little puffs; his face was already growing numb after the few minutes he'd been outside.

The door opened to reveal a thin boy with a particularly owlish expression. Pale, bangs hanging past the frames of his glasses, the youngster shook the hair out of his face and examined the man standing behind the storm door. "Yes?"

"I'm Alexander Leeds."

"Mr. Leeds? Great!"

Alex attempted to hide his surprise. It had never occurred to him that Olivia had a child. Perhaps this was a neighbor's kid, hired to walk the dog or something. "I believe I have an appointment with Olivia Bennett."

The boy nodded, plainly checking him out. "Okay." He held open the storm door and let Alex inside. "She'll be ready in a minute."

Alex let the warmth of the house surround him—a wood stove blazed in the corner of a incredibly rumpled living room. Newspapers were piled in odd areas on the maroon carpet, and the faded tan sofa "pit" looked like a candidate for a major yard sale. Alex liked that. It meant that Olivia had the wisdom to put her money into her product, instead of luxuries that could come later.

The boy didn't offer to take his coat, but Alex shrugged off the heavy cashmere and laid it gingerly over the back of a bright green rocking chair. "I take it no one else has arrived yet?"

"No one else?"

"Isn't there a board meeting?"

"Oh, yeah," the boy agreed, understanding reflected in his blue eyes. He grinned. "They're all around here somewhere."

"Good." Alex glanced at his watch. Four o'clock precisely. The boy stuck out his hand. "I'm Josh Bennett, Mr. Leeds. It's a pleasure to meet you."

Bennett? Warning bells sounded, but Alex kept his expression neutral as he shook the boy's hand. "Nice to meet you too, Josh."

"I've prepared a financial statement and a rough projection of Fancy's distribution potential. Would you like to go over them before the meeting?"

What did a kid—Olivia's kid?—know about distribution potential? Alex frowned. He wasn't about to discuss business with a child. "I think I'll wait."

Josh's face fell, but he quickly recovered. "We've got everything set up. Sit down and I'll go tell 'em you're here."

Alex heard the music stop and the low murmur of a woman's voice. All noise came to a halt. He sat alone in the rocking chair and wondered if he was being set up for a practical joke. Josh returned with a wary teenager behind him. The boy was extremely tall—Alex guessed six-five, easy—and his hair was dark, wavy and long. His jeans were a long way from new, and the sleeves of his black sweatshirt were rolled up to reveal wiry forearms. He didn't smile when he offered his hand. "I'm Wolf." "Wolf?"

"John Wolfgang Bennett. It's a family name." His eyes challenged Alex to ask any questions. Alex stood up to shake the giant's hand and wondered what he'd gotten himself into. Perhaps Olivia was the boy's aunt.

"Wolf," he repeated. "I'm Alexander Leeds."

"Yeah, " the boy answered coolly. "We know."

Before Alex could decide whether or not to leave, the petite blonde he'd been waiting for hurried into the room. "Alex." She smiled, holding out a small hand. "It's good to see you again. Thank you for coming."

"Olivia." He took her hand in a brief clasp and hated to let her go. Alex usually preferred tall women, sleek brunettes especially, but once again the dynamo with the curling yellow hair and big blue eyes stunned him. Instead of the exquisite black sheath he remembered, she wore snug, faded jeans. He couldn't decide which he preferred. A buttery-yellow sweater enhanced her sexy body, but she seemed unaware of it. No sophisticated hairdo this afternoon, though the wavy hair made her look like a blond gypsy. Glittery yellow earrings dangled from her ears, and Alex had no doubt that she'd made them herself. "You're wearing a Fancy Nancy?"

"What?"

"You're wearing Fancy Nancy earrings."

"Yes." She sounded nervous. He wondered if she'd had second thoughts about having him represent her company. Somehow the thought aggravated him. "We're glad you came."

He was beginning to be glad, too. He barely registered the fact that this lovely woman was the mother of the giant called Wolf. She barely looked twenty-five. Maybe these children were her stepchildren. Or her nephews. He quickly amended the thought when a miniature replica of Olivia bounded in and threw herself onto the sofa. "Hi!" She grinned at Alex. "How long is this gonna take?"

Alex didn't have the remotest idea and opened his mouth to say so.

"Shut up," Wolf ordered, glaring at his sister as he said it.

"Get off my stuff!" Josh yelled.

"Get a life," Nancy muttered, but she hopped off the couch and tried to smooth the rumpled papers. Alex turned his back on the squabble and faced Olivia.

"Obviously you've met my children."

Suspicion confirmed. Too bad. He never dated women with children. In fact, it was his number one rule. He swallowed his disappointment and lifted his briefcase. It was obviously time for some privacy, time to get down to business and away from the distractions. He smiled his most charming smile, the one designed to hide his true feelings. "Yes. Now where can we talk?"

"In the dining room," she said. "This way." He started to follow her, then realized the children were heading in the same direction. A nasty suspicion niggled in his brain. "Where are the other board members?"

"This is it. I mean, these are them."

"*This* is the board of directors?"

Olivia smiled. "What were you expecting?"

"Adults," he muttered under his breath. He followed her out of the snug living room, reluctant to leave the warmth of the wood stove, but anxious to get this meeting over. He didn't work with children; if he'd wanted to do that, he would have become a schoolteacher, for heaven's sake. Or gotten married and had his own. Neither idea held any appeal.

The dining room table was set up for a conference. Five places had been prepared but, unlike any other conference table Alex had seen, a bowl of potato chips and a platter of cookies sat in the middle. An enormous amount of clutter stood precariously stacked in each corner. The same maroon carpet stretched throughout this room; its white walls were covered with family photographs. Alex smelled coffee and would have given fifty dollars to have a cup of the stuff appear before him.

Josh pointed to a chair at the foot of the table. "That's yours."

Alex moved to sit down, noting that his was the only place that had a square blue paper box in front of it. "What's this?"

The boy smiled, making himself look even younger. "Oh, that's what you're going to tell us how to sell."

Alex didn't bother to open it. He had four pairs of Fancy Nancy earrings in the car. Each store he'd visited had said the same thing: the earrings sold well and were popular with girls. Still, Alex knew a fad when he saw one and believed himself smart enough not to get involved. However, he remained determined to be polite, so he put his briefcase upon the table and snapped it open, then took a yellow legal pad and a pen from its neatly organized contents.

Olivia sat down across from him at the head of the table. "This is a family-owned business, Mr. Leeds. I thought that was explained to you."

"I'm afraid I didn't take it literally."

"Your mistake," she said smoothly, as if she'd sensed the way he'd reacted to the children's presence and didn't appreciate it. Not one bit.

"Excuse me, but is there a *Mr.* Bennett available for this meeting?" *Is there anything else you neglected to tell me when we met?*

"No. There is no longer a Mr. Bennett." She didn't stop to give him an explanation, but gestured to her sons. "Let's introduce ourselves," she said to the kids. "Wolf, you start."

"I already did." There was a blatant warning in those dark eyes, and Alex felt like a bull who'd wandered onto the wrong ranch. "I'm vice-president."

"Okay," his mother said. "Josh?"

The boy grinned at Alex as if they were old friends. "I'm treasurer."

"Nancy?"

The little yellow-haired girl eyed him. "I'm Nancy Bennett. I think up stuff for the earrings."

"She's the creative director," Josh supplied.

Wolf rolled his eyes. "Could we get on with this? I have practice in an hour."

"Wolf . . ." his mother warned. She turned to Alex to explain, "Wolf is on the basketball team."

Not exactly a shock. Alex couldn't believe this entire meeting. It had to be someone's idea of a joke. But he sat still, waiting to decide how long it would take him to get out of this one.

"And I'm the president," Olivia told him. "We all work very hard. It was quite a Christmas season."

"You made all the earrings yourself? Here?"

"Yes, to both questions." She reached down beside her chair and pulled out a black velvet display of earrings in assorted sizes and colors. "Here's a sample of what we sell."

Alex barely glanced at them—he'd been looking at identical earrings all afternoon. "What makes you think you can go national with a product like this? From what I've seen, your product is more suited to craft shows and a few specialized boutiques."

"True, but the success of the earrings has given us other ideas," she answered.

The teenager slid over a paper to Alex. "Before we go any further with this, you'd better sign this agreement of confidentiality."

Alex scanned the standard document, took a pen from his pocket and scrawled his name on the bottom line. "There." He handed the paper back to Wolf. "Now why don't you tell me what you have in mind?"

"An earring-making kit," Olivia answered.

"What?"

"You have one in front of you. Open it."

Alex pulled the box toward him and slipped it open. Nestled inside were tiny plastic bags. He took each one out. They were filled with plastic rhinestones, jewelry hooks, metal shapes of hearts and flowers, earring backs, glitter and a small vial of white household glue. Alex put each bag in front of him on the table and lined them up in a neat row. He hadn't expected an earring kit, but excitement slowly uncurled from the pit of his stomach. Kits always had possibilities.

When he had emptied the box, he moved it out of the way and looked across the table once more. Olivia's big blue eyes held questions, but she managed to control her impatience. "Why don't you tell me about it?"

"I've been making earrings for two years," she began. "And the kids have been helping me. We started at the craft shows and then put them into gift shops. They're not expensive, and yet they attract attention."

Alex nodded. He'd heard the same thing from the store owners he'd talked to. "I thought you were going to market the earrings themselves."

"No." Olivia tapped the neatly printed financial statement in front of her. "As you can see, I don't think we're ready to risk money on the fashion business."

She was smart, Alex decided. And beautiful, in a domestic, fluffy kind of way. He preferred his women tall, sleek and independent. At least, he thought he did. But would she be easy to work with? He could afford to take his time and wait—he was in no hurry to screw up a perfect track record as the marketing whiz of New England. "Let's talk about why you think an earring kit would sell."

"Josh?"

Josh cleared his throat and turned to Alex. "There aren't any earring-making kits on the market right now. No one's thought of it but us, I think. We went to a whole bunch of toy stores and hobby shops, but the only kits are for making pot holders or weaving or that plastic stuff you melt in the oven to make ornaments."

Alex didn't have the faintest idea what the boy was talking about, but made a note to investigate the products mentioned. "Who wants to make earrings?"

"Me," Nancy answered. "I just love it." She turned to her mother. "I hafta go for a minute."

"Aside from Nancy." He addressed the question to Olivia as Nancy danced past him on her way out of the door.

"Geez!" Josh sighed. "Doesn't she ever stop going to the bathroom?"

"Shut up," Wolf said to his brother. "This is a business meeting."

"I know that!"

Olivia ignored the interruption and continued. "Little girls love to make their own jewelry. Especially earrings, because little girls love earrings." She absently touched the yellow and gold, glitter-dusted one on her earlobe. "Women do, too."

Alex struggled to keep his attention focused on the woman across from him. "Why do you think that?"

"I've tested it," she said. "On a lot of kids. It just snowballed. One day we were making earrings to sell and Nancy's friends were over and wanted to help, so all of a sudden we were letting kids make earrings, and they were having such a good time I thought it would be an idea to have a kit to sell. I put a few together, Nancy gave them as gifts, and they were a hit."

"It's an idea, all right." Alex tapped his pencil on the paper. "One that might be worth pursuing."

"What's the big deal?" Wolf demanded. "Either you like the idea or not."

"Wolf..." His mother's voice once again held a warning.

"No," Alex said. "He's right." He looked around the table. Josh was looking at him eagerly, Nancy had returned to her seat and was busily picking nail polish off her fingernails, and Olivia was looking at him with those gorgeous eyes of hers. Waiting. "What do you want from me?"

Olivia leaned forward. "I need a complete financial analysis of the business before we can get a loan from the bank. I've already had one bank turn me down."

"You can get an analysis from any accountant who deals with small business. Including Judd."

"I also need a marketing plan."

"A volunteer from the Small Business Association would give you one for free."

Olivia's lips tightened. "No." She looked at him— hard. "I checked up on you. You're the best in New England, maybe even the best east of the Mississippi. I figure that for a percentage—"

"A small percentage," Josh interrupted. "To be agreed on by the board."

"That's us," Nancy informed him.

Olivia continued. "For a percentage, you'd have enough at stake to help Fancy Nancy become a national product. We know it can work, and I don't have enough money for this to drag on forever. Wolf's a junior already and will need college tuition. My job pays the bills—barely—but there's nothing left over for anything else. I don't have years to watch a product grow. I don't have three years to get in the black. I have to hit hard and fast and big, if I'm going to do this thing at all."

"You're asking for a lot," he told her, but inwardly he smiled. If not for the children and this terribly unconventional household, Olivia would be the perfect client, at least for him. Unfortunately for his plans for this evening, she was no longer the perfect woman. Disappointing, but one of life's realities.

"And what are you asking for?"

"You're assuming I'm interested."

"I think you are," she said softly. "Or you wouldn't still be sitting here."

He inclined his head. "That's not necessarily true, Mrs. Bennett."

"Olivia."

"Fine, Olivia." He leaned back and crossed one long leg over the other. "A percentage of the profits is possible. Plus expenses."

"What kind of expenses?"

"Phone, mailing, travel, et cetera."

She frowned. "No. I have no control over your expenses and I don't want to be responsible for them."

"We'll work it out."

"What does that mean?"

"It means that if we decide to work together, we'll work it out." He had no intention of discussing financial arrangements in front of three children.

Wolf leaned on the table and glared at Alex, then turned to his mother. "This is garbage, Mom. How do we even know he's worth it?"

"I did my research, too, honey. Mr. Leeds is the best money can buy."

She made him sound like a cleaning product. Alex wondered at the reason behind the boy's hostility but felt confident that he could work around the resentment he was hearing. He'd been a teenager himself, hadn't he?

Alex opened his briefcase with two decisive little clicks and took out a sheaf of papers. He slid it toward

Wolf. "Here. This gives you my background and credentials." Everyone was quiet as Wolf leafed through the papers. "As you can see," Alex continued, "I have extensive experience in new-product development and marketing. Ten years' worth, to be exact. I'm sure you'll recognize some of the name brands I've listed as credentials."

"Okay. So you're a big shot. What can you do for us—for Fancy Nancy?" Wolf tossed the papers aside and Josh lunged for them, grabbing the folder greedily.

"Wolf . . ." There was that warning tone in Olivia's voice again.

"I don't know, yet. I have to study your business idea carefully before I commit to it. If I don't think it will work, or if I don't think you're willing to accept my skills, then I'll ride off into the sunset while you decide what you want to do with your earring kit. But I won't be rushed. Fair enough?"

Wolf nodded his agreement.

"Fair enough," Olivia said, her voice smooth. She looked serene, unconcerned and even a little amused. "Would you like a tour of the plant?"

2

"Now?"

"Why not?" The small show of reluctance on Alexander's part didn't faze Olivia for one moment. She considered it a momentary setback, that was all. When he didn't answer, she pushed her chair back and stood.

"The meeting's over," she told the children. "Wolf, you're free to go to practice, but come home right afterward. Josh, you have a science paper to type, right?" He nodded and she continued. "Nancy, you need to clean your room and unload the dishwasher."

Her orders given, Olivia turned to Alex. "I think you'll enjoy seeing the operation. We converted the basement—"

"Look, Olivia, I think we may be wasting each other's time." He tucked the papers inside the briefcase, snapped it shut and stood. The Fancy Nancy Earring Kit remained on the table, although he saw that the cookies and potato chips had mysteriously disappeared.

Her blue eyes flashed. "I'm paying you for this consultation, aren't I?"

"No."

She frowned. "Of course I am."

He shook his head. "This is . . . a favor."

"No way. This is a business deal. Or that's what I thought it was at Judd's house." She didn't need his charity, for heaven's sake. Who did he think he was dealing with, anyway?

"I don't make business deals at parties."

Olivia felt a blush heat her cheeks. Their instant attraction to each other that night could have been her imagination, but she doubted it. She'd never thought of herself as the kind of woman to fall for the some-enchanted-evening routine, but she's been wrong. She'd had stars in her eyes for days afterward. Until doubt set in. Had he taken a lady friend on vacation with him? Had she, Olivia, simply been an amusing flirtation to liven up a holiday cocktail party?

The man was still frowning as he added, "Besides, how much of a business deal can this be when three kids are involved?"

"They are part of this company."

"Which may be your first mistake."

"I don't think so."

"Let's hope you're right, then." He ran one hand through his hair, presenting a charming picture of boyish, rumpled male. Olivia wasn't fooled, though. She'd heard the Leeds charm was legendary and didn't intend to fall for it again. Right now her business was at stake.

"Come on," she insisted. "Let me impress you with the factory."

He had no choice but to give her a chance. Or at least let her think he was giving her a chance. *Blueberries.* Her eyes were the identical shade of dusty blue. Alexander blinked. He hadn't thought of the wild blueberry bushes of his childhood in years. He followed her tantalizing little figure through the hall and down a narrow set of stairs. He inhaled nail polish fumes as he carefully negotiated the dim stairway, then stopped short at the sight in front of him.

"This is the workroom," Olivia explained unnecessarily. She waved one delicate hand toward a row of tables. "These are the earrings I painted this morning. They're drying."

Alex stepped up for a closer look. The earrings were being held in upside-down egg cartons, so the effect was one of an elementary school craft project. "You really sell all of these?"

Olivia looked insulted. "I wouldn't make them if we didn't. Oh," she added, with another wave of her hand, "we've had some failures, some colors or shapes that weren't popular with the customers, but mostly we've done fine."

"How long?"

"How long what?"

"How long have you been in this business?"

"Two years."

He bent to examine the contents of a cardboard box. "Where do you get your supplies?"

"A wholesaler in Johnston. They let me buy in small quantities."

"What's a small quantity?"

"One gross." She watched him explore the contents of the tables until she couldn't stand the silence any longer. "So, what do you think?"

Alex stared into a bucket of golden glitter. What did he think? He thought he was drowning, totally out of control. He had rules about dating women with children. They didn't have the freedom to travel, they always worried about baby-sitters, you could never spend the night, and he detested being assessed as a potential father.

So he'd made his rules. And lived quite happily by them, too. Until he turned around and looked into Olivia Bennett's exquisite face.

Blueberry eyes. Daffodil hair. Considering the windchill factor, it was probably fifteen below outside. It was the middle of January, and yet he could swear that spring was coming. Wasn't he standing right across from her? He could smell the flowers or he could run. Running sounded good. "I think we made plans to have dinner together in January," he heard himself say. "Are you free this evening?"

"Yes, but—"

"Good." Alex looked at his watch. "I'll pick you up at seven. That will give me time to read your financial reports." Within minutes he retrieved his briefcase, grabbed his coat, and escaped into the frigid January wind.

OLIVIA HADN'T INTENDED to say yes to Alex's invitation. She told herself it was a simple business dinner. No doubt Alex would write if off as a business expense, so she would look at it as an opportunity to discuss her product, not as a romantic continuation of their first meeting.

That encounter had knocked her socks off. "Watch it," Judd's wife had warned on the telephone the next morning. "He's gorgeous, charming and—according to Judd—totally unable to commit."

Well, she didn't want any commitments, either. She'd reassured Polly that her life didn't have room for one more person. Still, Olivia wanted to look her best this

evening, so she raced into action. Alex might be
spending his time between now and dinner reading financial reports, but she had more important things to
think about. She took another shower, redid her
makeup, and spent forty-five minutes twisting her hair
into shape before deciding to leave it down. She ironed
her black rayon skirt and steamed her blue silk jacket
and matching top.

Ridiculous, she told herself. The man was only interested in her company—she had *begged* him to be interested in her company—but still, she couldn't help
enjoying the thought of going out to dinner with Alex.
Despite his reputation. Despite his reluctance to become involved in her company because of the children. Despite the fact that he was totally wrong for her.

THE HOUSE REMAINED blissfully quiet. Wolf had gone
to the movies with his latest girlfriend, and Olivia had
bribed the other two children to stay in her room and
watch television instead of greeting Alex at the door
and making him nervous with their questions.

He was prompt, of course. She answered the door on
the second knock and stepped back to let him enter.
"Hello. Come on in."

"Gladly. I think the temperature's dropped ten degrees in the past hour."

"Really?" She lifted her coat from the back of the
rocking chair, but Alex was too quick for her.

"You look lovely," he murmured as he took her coat
and held it while she slipped her arms into the sleeves.

"Thank you." She stepped away from the suddenly
close contact. The touch of his hands on her shoulders
had left shivers. Ridiculous for her to behave this way.

"Do you like seafood?" he was saying.

"Love it."

"Good. I made reservations at Spain."

"That sounds wonderful." She scribbled a note for the children on the blackboard around the corner.

He darted a look around the empty living room as if he expected the children to leap from behind the sofa. "Where is everybody?"

"Busy watching TV. Wolf's out on a date, too."

She noticed he looked relieved. She picked up her flat evening purse and Alex opened the door for her. He kept his hand on her elbow as they walked down the steps. His mother had clearly taught him impeccable manners. No wonder he was so much in demand; the perfect bachelor. Olivia sighed inwardly. Perfect bachelors didn't take perfect mothers out to dinner unless it was a business deal.

He tucked her into his tiny sports car. Olivia rubbed her hands together for warmth. The little car was obviously very expensive, and she would like to feel some of that expensive heat hitting her body pretty soon.

Alex noticed her shivering. "Cold? It'll warm up in a moment."

"Do little cars like this have heat?"

"Of course they do." He fiddled with the electronic panel and a fan whirred quietly. "See?"

She didn't want to see it, she wanted to feel it, but Olivia kept quiet. It wouldn't do to antagonize him. She needed to prove they could work together. "Thank you. This is a very nice car."

"It's a 308 GTSI," he said with pride.

"I don't think I know what that means."

He patted the cream leather interior proudly. "She's a 1985 Ferrari. My one luxury."

She doubted he had only one luxury. "Well, she's beautiful." Especially now that "she" was providing heat. Olivia clasped her gloved hands in her lap. "I think we should get right down to business."

He grinned at her and put the car into gear. "Do we have to?"

"Isn't that the point of this dinner?"

Alex didn't answer right away. "Not especially. I would have invited you to dinner the night we met, but you had to decorate a Christmas tree."

"And now I have to find a marketing director for my company."

"Could we discuss this over drinks?"

She ignored his request. "Have you ever been married?"

"Is that a personal question or is it related to business?"

"Related to business." *Sort of.*

"No."

"I didn't think so. Children?"

"No," he stated more emphatically. "I believe in safe sex and birth control, if that's any of your business, which it really isn't. At least not tonight."

She chose to ignore the last remark. "Your sex life isn't my business, that's true." She couldn't believe she was discussing this. "But I do need to know what your experience is with children."

"No," he corrected. "You need to know what children's products I've represented in the past. It's all in the file I gave you this afternoon. The Weepy Wilma doll was one of mine. And I put in some marketing time at Hasbro before going out on my own."

"But you know what children like?"

"That's where the market research comes in." As if he could tell she wasn't convinced, he added, "I have a godchild in California."

"What did you give her for Christmas?"

Alex looked at her sharply. "What on earth does that have to do with anything?"

"How old is she?"

"Who?"

"Your godchild."

"Five." Alex drove the car toward the ocean. "And I bought her a book."

"Very nice. Was that your own idea?"

"No."

Olivia thought it wise to change the subject. "Did you grow up in Rhode Island?"

"In Providence. And you?"

"Here in South County. I never wanted to live anywhere else."

"I don't blame you," he said, guiding the car into the parking lot. "I spent summers in Narragansett and decided I had to live here when I grew up."

"It's changed a lot."

"I still like it." He switched off the engine and turned toward her in the dim interior. He was very, very close. The warm air enhanced the fragrance of his after-shave.

"Me, too." Olivia inhaled. She remembered that scent from the Christmas party.

Obviously in no hurry to leave the car's warmth, Alex smiled at her. He reached out and touched a strand of her hair. "I wondered what your hair would look like down. And this afternoon I found out."

This wasn't exactly a business conversation, but suddenly Olivia didn't mind. He was flirting with her again, instead of acting the reserved businessman as he had this afternoon. Once again he was the charming male who flattered her so easily. She liked this man better. "You discovered quite a few things about me this afternoon." There. Better to bring it out into the open.

"You don't look like a mother." He dropped his hand. "And I'm not exactly a family man."

"I could tell."

He shrugged, but his dark eyes were warm as he studied her. "I don't pretend to be anything I'm not."

"Ouch."

He looked surprised. "I didn't mean you did. You simply did not look . . . maternal the night we met."

"And now I do?"

He laughed. "Not exactly."

"I was told to watch out for your charm."

That didn't appear to faze him. "So? Watch out."

Alex looked as if he was going to kiss her. Olivia wouldn't have minded much if he had, but struggled to keep control of her common sense. It wouldn't do to get tangled up with Alexander Leeds. Right now she should be keeping her mind on Fancy Nancy, not on romance. She hesitated just a fraction, and saw his eyes darken.

"Hungry?"

"Yes." She knew he meant dinner. Of course he did. Olivia sighed. It had been an indecently long time since she'd even considered making love to anyone. She wondered if she remembered how it felt.

Heat burned her face. She remembered how it felt, all right. Olivia struggled to keep up her end of the conversation. "I've never been here before."

"You're in for a treat." He put his hand on the door. "One thing, Olivia."

"What?"

"No more talk about business until after dinner." He smiled again, his eyes crinkling at the corners. "It's a rule I have."

His eyes were the most wonderful shade of brown. Golden flecks, long lashes. Nice. "And you always follow the rules?"

"If they're my rules."

She liked his attitude.

SINCE IT WAS the off-season, they had the entire dining room almost to themselves. Romantic and quiet, the restaurant was dimly lit, and a glimpse of ocean could be seen across the seawall. They shared a bottle of sangria, and Olivia sampled the spicy appetizers Alex ordered. The waiter was young and handsome, attentive throughout their lobster dinner, and finally when Olivia sipped her coffee at the end of the meal, she became aware that they had put off the inevitable business discussion. It would be good to get it over, she told herself. Because one way or another, she'd know tonight if she had hired a marketing director.

"Well, Alex, do we discuss business now?"

He put his coffee cup back upon its saucer and looked reluctant. "I promised, didn't I."

"Not exactly. I think you simply followed your rules."

Time for reality, Alex decided. So much for the pleasant evening. "I have another rule, Olivia, and I think you already know what it is. I don't work with kids."

Her eyebrows rose. "I do."

"Look, just hear me out." He gave her his most sincere, I'm-only-doing-this-for-you look. "You need an adult board of directors. One that will work in your best interests."

She didn't look impressed by this expression of concern. In fact, she went very still, though her voice was soft. "My *best interests* are doing quite nicely. My children have worked hard for this company. Nights, weekends. They've done everything I've asked them to do."

"They wouldn't lose their jobs, Olivia, but it doesn't look good to have kids in directors' chairs."

"Is there a law against it?"

"No."

"Then they stay." She sipped her coffee and held his gaze. "And perhaps you don't."

"What's that supposed to mean?"

"If you don't like it—and can't accept it—then I'll have to find a marketing director who will."

They stared at each other for a long moment until Alex briefly looked away. "I don't get involved in hobbies."

Her blue eyes narrowed. "I don't have time for them either."

"There's a lot of money involved."

"There's a lot of money to be made."

He wouldn't argue with that, but he also knew how long it could take to get a product off the ground. "Look, you'll have to be realistic—"

"That's what I want to hire you for. To be realistic." She held his gaze again. "Look, I brought you to my home today to check out our idea, to see what you thought of Fancy Nancy as a product. So tell me. Do we have a viable product or not?"

"You do," he finally admitted. "It has possibilities."

"Then what's the problem? Don't you think you can market it?"

"Possibly."

"Then will you?"

"I don't know. It's not that simple."

"What's so difficult?"

"Look, Olivia, you have a good idea for a new product—maybe. Most new products fail because the company overestimated the need for the product or underestimated the competition or introduced the product too soon, before it was developed or tested properly." He looked at her intently to see if she was still listening. She was. "Or they fail because of a poorly planned marketing campaign."

"Which is where you come in."

"The best marketing plan in the history of sales will not sell something that consumers don't want."

Olivia looked doubtful. "What about pet rocks?"

"A fad," he replied. "That's a different ball game. Like money shredded in jars and slap bracelets. Here today and gone tomorrow."

"You sound negative."

"Realistic," he amended. "Remember, that's what you want me to be?"

"All right, so what do you want me to do?"

"The information you gave me this afternoon was just the start. I want you to explain to me how you're going to package the kit, how much each kit costs, who it will appeal to, how many times a year they will buy it, and your personal financial statement."

"Why do you need that?"

"I need to know how much you're risking, what you have to invest, and whether or not you'd be prepared to handle problems—financial and otherwise—as they come up. And they will, believe me."

"All right," she agreed after a long moment. "But you have to do something for me."

"What?"

"Go shopping."

"Why?"

Olivia felt oddly breathless. She brushed her hair from her face. "You have to see the gap we want to fill, right?"

"All right. Shopping it is. When?"

"The stores are open tomorrow afternoon. Are you free?"

He looked at her for another long moment. "I can be."

"Good. We have a deal."

"Not until we sign the contract. There's no turning back—for either of us—once we do."

"Yes. I'm aware of that." She smiled, a slow, sweet smile that threatened to rob his lungs of air.

"Good." Throughout the rest of the evening, as he paid the bill and drove Olivia back to her house, Alex had the uncomfortable feeling he'd been outmaneuvered. Still, he'd never been able to resist a challenge, and the Fancy Nancy Kit was definitely on the same level as an Olympic challenge. The benefits could be extraordinary, but he didn't want to get Olivia's hopes up. It would take planning, strategy and timing. And luck—although he personally thought luck was grossly overrated.

"HE'S EXTREMELY...attractive," Olivia conceded, stretching the telephone cord to its maximum length so she could remove her coffee cup from the microwave oven. "And knowledgeable," she added. "He knows what he's doing."

"It's not him I'm worried about," Polly said. "Alexander Leeds always knows what he's doing. I don't know him well, he's one of Judd's friends from way back when, but his life-style is not exactly *your* life-style."

"Well, that's true. He picked me up in his Ferrari and I didn't even know what it was." Olivia chuckled, and took a sip of her coffee.

"Forget the Ferrari. Do you recognize seduction when you see it coming?"

"It wasn't that kind of evening," Olivia fibbed. "We talked business."

"Which I'll bet wasn't his idea, was it?"

"Well, no, but we did get a lot settled about Fancy Nancy. He had a lot of questions about the business and I had a few questions about him."

"And?"

"We're going to toy stores today so I can show him how the kit will fit in."

"What did he do when he met the kids?"

"Practically fainted, but he was very, very cool."

"He can afford to be," Polly drawled. "Still, perhaps he can be domesticated. It might be interesting to see if it can be done. Maybe it's time Alex settled down."

"I don't want to domesticate anyone, least of all Alex Leeds. I have no intention of getting personally involved," Olivia insisted. "I simply want to make a lot of money."

"Aside from the making money part, there's nothing wrong with dating a handsome, charming man. Even mothers can have some fun, you know."

"Not this mother," Olivia said. "I have other things on my mind." *Like survival.*

Polly sighed. "All right, I give up. Call me sometime next week and let me know if you hired him."

"Sure. But don't say anything to Judd, will you? I don't want to have to talk about this at the office tomorrow. Judd's always trying to fix me up, and he'd love to know all about this."

"Don't worry. We're going into tax season, remember? Judd won't even know what planet he's on until April 15."

Olivia knew that was true. She'd been one of Judd McCann's secretaries for five years, and every tax season was busier than the one before. The usually easy-going accountant would alternate between stressing calm organizational procedures and rushing from office to office, asking everyone to work late. Olivia said goodbye to her friend and hung up the phone. She filled her cup from the carafe and stared into the quiet dining room. Everyone but her was sleeping late this Sunday morning, and Olivia enjoyed the peace. In a few moments she would add some logs to the wood stove and collect the Sunday paper from the front steps, but for now she would just lean against the counter and savor being alone.

It was easy for Polly to suggest she go out with handsome bachelors once in a while, but her friend didn't understand what it was like to be alone and responsible for three other lives, too. Handsome, charming Alex Leeds would only complicate matters, and as much as she wished she'd never asked him to consider representing Fancy Nancy, there was no way she could back out now.

3

"THIS STORE is incredible," Alex said, surveying the well-stocked aisles of toys. "Weepy Wilma sold out during the Christmas of '86."

Olivia didn't share his enthusiasm. "I remember that Christmas. I was one of the mothers who stood in line one Monday morning for the privilege of spending $22.50 on a doll that cried voice-activated tears."

Alex grinned as they navigated the crowded aisles of Toys 'R' Us. "I like to hear that. Someday I'll tell you how we did it." Alex was pleased with himself. Olivia had wanted to meet him here in Warwick, at the giant Toys 'R' Us store near the Rhode Island Mall. But he'd insisted on picking her up. The Ferrari held only two people, and he'd been determined to avoid the rest of the board of directors joining the excursion and terrorizing the toy store. After all, this was supposed to be a business meeting. Alex hid his satisfied smile. Mission accomplished. Thirty-five minutes after he'd collected Olivia, they were walking through the giant toy store without another Bennett in sight.

"Here," she said, pointing to an aisle. "This is where I think Fancy Nancy should be."

Fancy Nancy. He had to do something about that name. They turned left and stared silently at the shelves of children's craft supplies and kits.

"See?" she said. "We're a few steps up from pop-it beads, but there's nothing else on the shelves like Fancy Nancy."

"I see what you mean." He pulled a small spiral notebook from his jacket pocket and made some notes on prices, packaging and manufacturers. So far what she'd told him was true. There was room for her product in the marketplace, and from what he'd read in yesterday's report, the cost of putting the kit together might be low enough to factor in the marketing, shipping and insurance she'd need to get her idea off the ground. If his guess was correct, there'd be a healthy profit margin left over.

"Well?"

"Well, what?" Alex looked up from his pad and saw Olivia with her hands on her hips. She was wearing a yellow turtleneck shirt and jeans again. He was becoming very partial to those jeans. He had promised himself he would resist her, resist the dusty-blue eyes and the blond hair, which was pulled into a respectable knot at the back of her neck. He'd told himself he would pretend she was his sister, his elementary school teacher or even the wife of an acquaintance.

"Do you try to keep me in suspense all the time?"

She looked nothing like anyone he'd ever met before. Alex flipped the cover over his pad and tucked it with his pen into his shirt pocket. "Sorry. I didn't mean to." He took her elbow. "C'mon. Let's go next door to the mall and have lunch. We'll talk there."

"I don't really have the time. I still have a lot of work to do at home."

"A quick cup of coffee, then."

"Well, all right. There's another toy store I'd like to show you."

"Good," he agreed, walking down the aisle of Barbie dolls. "Do you ever buy these for, uh, your daughter?"

"Nancy? Sure."

"Amazing, isn't it?" They paused in front of the display; the trademark pink color dominated one side of the aisle from floor to ceiling. "How many of these does Nancy own?"

"At least a dozen."

"And they put more out each year. Brilliant," he muttered. "No one's been able to touch them for years."

"I still have mine. And all of her clothes."

Alex nodded. "That's what I mean. The attachment to these dolls is eerie."

"No, it's not." She picked up a Birthday Girl Barbie and examined it closely. "Everyone loves her gorgeous clothes. Little girls love to comb her hair, too."

"Plus the fact that she's a blonde and blue-eyed."

"Not all of them." She pointed to another Birthday Girl Barbie, who was black, and then to an Oriental Barbie Rocker with a long fall of black hair.

"The rest of them look like you," Alex noted.

She looked over at him. "I don't! I mean, they do not."

He picked up a box directly in front of him and with a smug smile held it up for Olivia's perusal. "They don't?"

This particular Barbie wore jeans, and her yellow hair was fuller and wavier. Her heavily made-up eyes were blue, and tiny plastic rhinestones sparkled in her tiny plastic earlobes. "I don't see the resemblance.

And—" Olivia smiled "—they don't make short Barbie dolls." She turned away from him and his silly teasing. The assortment of dolls dazzled her, and she eyed the many different kinds of outfits they wore. Nancy's birthday was coming up in a couple of weeks. Maybe Birthday Barbie was just the thing.

Alex stepped away from the pink boxes. "I thought women hated these dolls."

"Well, some do find them offensive. You know, the large breasts, tiny waist and long legs, which are what the American woman has possibly been brainwashed to—oh, forget it, Alex. Barbie is just a pretty doll. Little girls like the glamorous outfits and the long hair to brush."

"You have that shopper look. Are you actually going to buy one of these? Contribute to the Mattel dynasty and the brainwashing of future generations of American women?"

"Possibly." She ignored his teasing. The price of Birthday Barbie was higher than the amount she wanted to spend, but she didn't plan to tell Alexander Leeds, Ferrari owner, of that particular problem, even if he would soon know everything about her financial affairs. "Nancy's birthday is in a few weeks. She's having an earring-making birthday party and inviting all her little friends. In fact, it would be a perfect opportunity for you to see firsthand how the kit works."

He backed up a step. "I doubt—"

"Actually, it's a good idea." She eyed him with a speculative look, and Birthday Barbie was forgotten for a moment. "You need to see how this appeals to children, don't you?"

"Actually, you've described it very well."

"But there's nothing like firsthand experience." Those blue eyes assessed him, and he could tell by her expression that she expected him to refuse.

"You may be right," he conceded. "Can we discuss this over coffee?"

"What are you afraid of, Alex? A few children and a couple of bowls of glitter?"

"That's ridiculous. *If* I decide to take you on as a client, I'll decide how much I need to be involved." He glared at her. "And I'll decide whether or not to supervise the creative department's activities."

"Oh, don't be so stuffy, Alex. You'll have fun."

"No one has ever called me stuffy." His voice was mild. "Charming, of course. Intelligent, often." She looked at him as if she didn't know he was teasing. Alex headed toward the front of the store and Olivia followed him into an available checkout lane.

Trapped. He'd been trapped once again. He wondered if he could become accustomed to the feeling. Somehow Olivia had managed to ensnare him in her plans, her family, her business. Which, of course, was why he'd always successfully avoided becoming involved in any way, shape, or form with domestic, maternally minded women.

He'd been right all along, he told himself. He'd better get out now while he could. Even if it meant turning his back on a potential gold mine.

Olivia paid for the doll, then buttoned her coat as Alex stood beside her. All right; she shouldn't have called him stuffy. It wasn't the kindest or even the most tactful thing she could have said, but the man did have a way of annoying her. He was so damn sure of himself all the time.

She followed him to the door, which opened electronically as they approached. "Are you going to the mall next?" Olivia pulled her collar high over her ears and hurried to keep up with Alex's long strides across the parking lot. "There's another store there you should see."

"Lunch first," he said, opening the car door for her. She was amazed that he continued to insist on opening doors, although she figured he was probably afraid she'd hurt the Ferrari ABC or GHI or whatever it was if she actually touched it with her own hands.

"I really don't need lunch," she said as he settled himself behind the steering wheel.

"I do."

She looked at her watch. "It's after two. I need to get home soon."

"I'll eat fast."

Olivia started to explain that she really didn't have time for lunch, but Alex's attention stayed on his driving. In minutes he'd driven across one parking lot and into the larger one on the south side of the Rhode Island Mall. He parked far away from any other cars, which Olivia assumed was so that no other metal would scrape the sides of his precious automobile.

Olivia made a point of looking around the empty spaces beside the car. "We could have taken my car, you know. It might have made parking a little easier."

"I thought about it, until I saw your car."

She hurried to open the door herself. "What does that mean?"

He waited for her to step around the Ferrari. "I didn't want to spend the day stuck along the side of Route 95, waiting for a tow truck."

"The Buick isn't that bad."

His eyebrows rose. "They wouldn't have found our bodies until spring."

She smiled at him. "Make me a rich woman so I can buy a new car."

He didn't answer until they'd navigated the windy parking lot. "I'm going to give it my best shot," he said, pulling the door open for her.

"Is that a commitment?"

"I have to read your reports."

"You'd better—I worked on them for two hours last night." Warmth and the aromas of cooking greeted them as they stepped inside the busy eating area.

"Food first." He selected a table near the delicatessen counter. "Are you sure you won't change your mind and have something to eat?"

Olivia eyed the display of cookies behind the glass. "Well . . ."

"Turkey club on white," he said to the woman behind the counter. "And a root beer, please. Two cups of coffee and . . ." He turned back to Olivia.

"A sugar cookie." Alex she could resist; cookies she couldn't.

He shot her a quick, sexy smile before turning back to the waitress. "Make that three cookies. Thanks."

Olivia sat down, unbuttoned her coat, and pulled the wire chair closer to the round table. Somehow she had to get him to discuss business. She wanted to stop fooling around with "maybe" and get right on with the money making part of her plan. In minutes Alex plunked a loaded plastic tray upon the table.

Olivia waited until he had finished arranging the food, disposed of the tray and shrugged off his coat. "I brought the papers you wanted with me."

Alex pried the lid from the coffee cup. "That was fast."

"I'm in a hurry, remember?"

He dumped three packets of sugar into his cup and stirred the mixture with a plastic spoon. "I've noticed."

The Bachelor of the Month couldn't possibly understand the kind of responsibility she felt twenty-four hours a day. That wasn't his fault, she understood, but it certainly didn't make her life any easier. She decided not to comment, opened up her coffee and took a tentative sip. It was going to take some time to cool, so she reached for the wax paper bag and selected a cookie.

"Sure you don't want to share this sandwich?"

Olivia eyed the large roll stuffed with lettuce and turkey. "I'm positive, but thanks for dessert."

He nodded and started to eat the sandwich. It was interesting to watch him, Olivia decided. He attacked the sandwich with a single-minded force that defied description. She broke the large cookie in half and let a bite melt in her mouth. She never had time to bake anymore. Ice cream, easily scooped into bowls, was the official dessert in the Bennett family, especially now that the earring business took up all of her spare time.

Alex finished the last bite, wiped his mouth, drained the root beer in one long swallow and tested his coffee. "That was a perfect lunch," he declared. "You don't know what you missed."

"You must have been hungry. Didn't you eat breakfast?"

Alex smiled at her over the rim of the coffee cup. "I don't cook."

"I guess you're too busy."

"It's a matter of priorities."

"I'm going to eat another one of these," she said, pulling a second cookie from the bag.

"Do you have anything you want to do here in the mall?"

"Besides the toy store?"

"Yeah." He sipped his coffee. "You know, new panty hose, a pair of shoes, a jacket to go with the skirt you bought on sale last month?"

Olivia thought he'd lost his mind. "I didn't come all the way up here to Warwick to do errands. And I don't need any of those things." *Except a new fitted sheet for my bed and some pillows to spruce up the old couch.*

"It's January. White sale time."

"I really don't have the time. . . ."

"I intend to sit here, drink my coffee and read the information you brought me. You did bring it, didn't you?"

She took a thick packet of folded papers from her purse and handed them to Alex. "I hope it's what you wanted."

He started to unfold them, then looked back at her. "Go ahead, Olivia. Come back in half an hour and we'll talk business."

"Okay." She stood up. "I'll leave my coat."

He didn't look as if he'd heard her, so she left the coat on the chair and picked up her purse. She looked at her watch. Thirty minutes in the mall wasn't a very long time, but if that was the way he wanted to do business, then she'd have to play along.

She returned in twenty-nine minutes, with the new sheet and without the pillows. Alex looked up and smiled. He put down his pen and leaned back in the chair.

"Tell me what you bought."

"Why?" It suddenly seemed like an intimate purchase. "Just a sheet."

His eyebrows rose. "May I see?"

"Why?"

"Curious, that's all."

She felt foolish making a federal case out of it, so she slipped the flat package from the bag. The sheet was patterned in a soft blue and white pinstripe dotted with roses and tulips.

"Very feminine," he observed. "It fits you."

"I like flowers."

"Yes, I—" he began, then stopped. He tapped the papers on the table. "I read through your papers. Between this and the figures your son gave me yesterday, your information is very complete."

Great. On to business. Olivia slid the sheet back into the bag. "I did what you asked."

"It could work," he said, still concentrating on the papers in front of him. "Your son—Josh, is it?" He glanced up, saw Olivia nod, and continued. "Josh put together an interesting amount of information for the meeting yesterday."

"He wants to be a business tycoon."

"He has a good start. I'm impressed."

It was silly to feel so pleased. "I'll tell him."

Alex hesitated and Olivia waited, her stomach tightening into a nervous tangle. "I'll work up a contract," he finally declared.

"We have a deal? You're taking Fancy Nancy on as a client?"

Alex looked directly into Olivia's eyes, and she caught herself before she thought one single unprofessional thing about Alexander Leeds. He was too gorgeous.

Alex smiled one of those charming smiles she figured he must have practiced when he was younger. "Yes, Olivia. I'm all yours."

ALL HERS? Fat chance. Olivia shut the basement door and went to one of the worktables. She turned on a light and sat down on a metal chair in front of a box of heart-shaped findings. She's sit here and paint a few earrings—a good way to avoid thinking about Alexander P. Leeds, a legend in his own time. He was an incorrigible flirt, with those laughing eyes and that slow smile. Imagine wanting to look at the bed sheet she'd bought, as if he needed to give her an opinion!

Olivia smiled and reached for the poppy-red nail polish. Valentine earrings should sell well next month, and it wouldn't hurt to have plenty on hand. Keeping busy usually kept her from thinking about the other things in her life—like Wolf's silences and how to pay the bills. And loneliness. She positively refused to feel lonely. She had three children, didn't she? But she had to admit she enjoyed some male attention in her life. Five years had passed since Jack left, promising an amicable custody settlement and child support if she'd give him a painless divorce. Painless for him, he'd meant. He'd had some sort of midlife crisis, suddenly wanting to quit his job as an accountant and backpack through Yellowstone Park.

Olivia had been willing to give him the space to do that, without the divorce, until she'd discovered a nineteen-year-old "hiking partner" figured in the mid-life crisis. One of those Amazon redheads with strong calves Jack had met at his health club. But Jack and the Amazon had never made it to Yellowstone—he'd dropped dead of a heart attack within sight of the Rocky Mountains.

So Olivia supposed she wasn't technically a divor-cée, since she'd actually been widowed before the final papers had been signed, but she still felt abandoned in more ways than she could count.

She didn't like to think about it, because she'd feel sorry for herself. Although how anyone could feel sorry for herself when she had three gorgeous, smart and tal-ented children . . .

She'd had occasional dates, usually a client of Judd's. But none of them had had the wicked gleam or flirty smile that Alex possessed.

Being with him was safe—safe because she knew he flirted with everyone. Olivia finished the first coat on the little heart, settled it into a holder to dry and reached for another. She could sit down here as long as she liked; the children were busy with their schoolwork, having left it until Sunday evening. The leftover ham-burger casserole could be heated in the microwave by anyone who had hunger pangs.

Olivia admired the earrings and continued to work. It might be the last peaceful evening she'd enjoy for a while. Alexander Leeds had signed a contract to rep-resent Fancy Nancy. Life would never be quite the same again.

SOMETIMES life wasn't fair. Alex tied his tie and examined his reflection carefully as he leaned toward the bathroom mirror. Of course, he'd never been taught life was fair, especially after he was eight years old, but still... There was always the hope that one day he'd find out differently.

He was still waiting. Alex grabbed the brush and quickly tamed his hair. He didn't care to spend a lot of time on his appearance, but he did take care of his clothes, as he took care of all his possessions. He'd make sure the mirror was clean, but wouldn't spend much time looking into it.

What was he going to do about Olivia? The woman had three children. She was also sexy as hell, which didn't quite go with the maternal image. He couldn't figure it out. Whenever he was with her, all he could think of was flowers and springtime and rolling around in a field of daisies with Olivia's naked body joined to his.

And it was only a Friday evening in January. What would he do when the first March breezes smelled of violets and the promise of a sunny day enveloped him? The earrings would be the first thing he'd take off her, that he knew. He promised himself there'd be no reminders of the business that had brought them together. But still, what was he going to do? How could he find out what attracted him to her unless he spent more time with her? There should be a logical way to figure this thing out.

He could take her out a few times. Get her out of his system. He could pretend the children didn't exist.

That was a good idea. It cheered him, so he flipped off the bathroom light switch and went down the narrow hall to the kitchen. He could either ignore the children or merely step around them, as if they were miniscule roadblocks. Alex frowned. The basketball player didn't look as if he would be any kind of minuscule roadblock, but Nancy and Josh would be easy to sidetrack. He would have to come up with a plan.

He was good at making plans.

FRIDAY WAS NOT the best night for a meeting, but Alex had insisted and Olivia had given in. It was his first night free all week, and there were some important things to go over before he really got started on the project. Also, on Friday it would be logical to invite Olivia out for a casual drink or dinner after the meeting. That strategy had worked well before.

He settled himself in the chair while Olivia called the meeting to order and waved to him to start talking.

"The name's wrong," he pronounced, and continued as if he'd just said, *"The month is January."*

"What?" three voices cried. Wolf said nothing, just frowned at his mother and turned back to Alex. They were grouped around the dining room table again, and Alex held a sheaf of papers before him.

He looked up, as if surprised that he'd created such an uproar. "The name Fancy Nancy sounds silly."

Nancy glared at him. "It is not!" she protested. "And Mom promised it would be named after me."

"That's true," Olivia agreed. "I promised."

"This isn't Girl Scout camp," he countered. "This is a business decision, a marketing issue." He smiled at Nancy. "It's nothing personal."

The child looked thoughtful, but Olivia continued to argue. "I don't think that's your decision to make."

"Okay," he said. "Let's get back to that discussion after we go through the rest of this."

Josh shot his mother a worried look, then leaned forward. "Good idea."

As Alex continued to question the color choices and sizes for the kits, the children had answers for him. Olivia let each one discuss the pros and cons of each of Alex's suggestions for change, but she didn't really like them. Who did he think he was, anyway?

She tried to stifle her feelings—after all, she had hired him to do this exact thing, hadn't she?—but some of the changes he wanted rankled. He cut the earring kit colors down to three and produced documentation to prove what colors attracted children, then expanded the amount of silver and gold glitter enclosed in each kit, and went on to discuss the cost of each component included in the package.

Olivia watched her children. Wolf listened as if waiting for Alex to say the wrong thing—something stupid that would give him a reason to throw the consultant out of the house. Josh hung on every word, following the points raised with greedy interest. Nancy fidgeted on her chair, but chimed in whenever colors were discussed. Alex kept his face expressionless, Olivia noticed. He acted as if he were talking to fifty-year-old board members and fully expected them to follow his facts and figures with no problem.

And the funny thing was, they seemed to do it. Olivia didn't know if they were faking or not, but it was a good act if they were. Wolf even relaxed long enough to ask a few intelligent questions—nonthreatening ones, even. And Alex answered them with unfaltering logic. They agreed on the percentage of the profits that he would take, plus a reasonably low figure on expenses.

Impressive, Olivia thought. But what about the name?

"There," Alex said. "I think that takes care of everything, except the glue supplier, and I'll work on that this week. I have someone I can call."

"What about the name?" Olivia said.

"Your mother and I will work up the official loan proposal for the bank."

"The name," Olivia repeated. "We should talk about it."

Alex straightened the pile of papers and set them down. He folded his hands in front of him. "We need a name that's flashy, something people will remember. Fancy Nancy could be any kind of product at all. There's no purchaser identification."

"I suppose you have an alternative."

"Just one."

"Which is?"

"Glitter Girl. But you may have others." He waited, but when on one responded, he continued. "It emphasizes the glitter, and the girl is your consumer, right? And you've been telling me how much little girls love glitter, right?"

"Right."

"Then let's hit them over the head with it, so to speak." He spread his hands in an open gesture. "Anyone else have any ideas?"

Silence greeted them, broken only by Nancy's grumbling, "But Mom promised."

"She's right. I did."

Alex looked around the table. The boys glared at him as if he were breaking the family into pieces with an ax. Obviously it was time for a compromise. "Perhaps— and I'm just tossing this idea out off the top of my head," he warned "—we could put Nancy's picture on the box. Instead of her name. It might work, though we won't know until we're ready for the cover design. But it is a possibility." The little girl's appealing blue eyes and golden hair would photograph well, he hoped. God, how he hoped!

Nancy didn't look convinced. "You promise?"

"No promises," he said. "I can't make promises unless I'm sure I can keep them. This was just an idea, but I'm willing to work on it."

"We could vote," Josh said. He looked to Alex. "Right?"

"Right."

"Secret ballots?"

Alex hid his smile. "If you think that's necessary."

"It's more fair," Nancy agreed. "Anybody got a pencil I can borrow?"

Alex turned to Josh. "You're the secretary." Josh passed out paper and within a minute the papers were returned.

Olivia refused the paper. "As chairman of this board, I'm not allowed to vote except in a tiebreaker."

Nancy bounced on her chair. "That's not fair."

Alex said, "I'm sure we could make an exception."

"No. We're in business now and we may as well act official."

He nodded. "All those in favor of changing the name of the product to Glitter Girl say aye. Or nay, for no."

Josh raised his hand. "You mean *write* it."

"Oh, fine, if that's what you want. A secret ballot."

Josh turned to the family. "*Write* aye or nay, then."

Nancy frowned and bit her pencil. "How do you spell that?"

"A-Y-E."

"Not that—the other one."

Alex didn't so much as blink. "N-A-Y."

Olivia watched them write quickly and fold their ballots.

"You have to give them to me," Josh said. "It's my job to count."

Alex sighed and leaned back in his chair, hands behind his head. Obviously he was accustomed to the corporate voting process. Olivia felt her left temple begin to pound and wondered when this meeting would end. She thought of her darkened bedroom and comfortable, queen-size mattress; how wonderful it would be to lie down on her bed and close her eyes for a few minutes. Instead she forced herself to sit up straight and to look patient while her son counted the ballots.

"Mr. Secretary?" she prodded after endless moments of silence. "Do we have the vote?"

"Three aye, one nay. They ayes have it. The name is changed to Glitter Girl."

"I knew it," Nancy moaned. "Nothing good ever happens to me."

Her brothers ignored her. Wolf stood up and looked at his mother. "Is this meeting over now?"

Olivia looked across the table to Alex. "I make a motion."

He nodded. "Seconded."

"Meeting adjourned," she declared. "Everyone in favour?" The board of directors showed their support by leaving the table.

"That went well," Alex said, putting papers into his briefcase.

"Are you surprised?"

"Actually, yes." He pushed the case aside and leaned back in his chair. "I was prepared for a fight over the name."

"I could still give you one, if you're disappointed."

"No, thanks. I believe I'll quit while I'm ahead." He looked at his watch. "Not quite six-thirty. We accomplished a lot in record time."

Olivia stood up. "I have to run."

"Why?"

"Dinner...."

"I'd like to take you out. We could celebrate...."

She didn't let him finish. "Wolf has a home game tonight. I have to throw something in the oven before we go to the gym."

"Basketball at six-thirty? Isn't that early?"

"He has to be there before seven, and we only have one car, so we're all going to the game together."

"I could give you a lift."

"In your little car? I don't think that would work." Alex knew she was right. He couldn't believe he'd offered. But he couldn't believe his careful plans were disintegrating, either.

"Besides," she continued, sweeping the business papers off the table and into a corner on the floor, "I don't think microwave pizza is your idea of dinner."

That irked him. She thought he was spoiled and picky. So what if she was right? "I could be the micro-

wave king of Rhode Island," he countered. "You'd never
even know, would you?"

That got a smile out of her. "I'd have a pretty good
idea. Are you also telling me you like basketball?"

"Season tickets to the Boston Celtics."

"These aren't the Celtics," she said, slipping into the
kitchen. He followed her and watched as she opened the
freezer compartment of the refrigerator and removed
four brightly colored boxes. "And this isn't real pizza."

"And this isn't an invitation to stay to dinner?" His
voice was light—he knew when he should retreat.

"No. Sorry."

"You don't have to apologize." She started to peel the
first cardboard strip from the box, but Alex stepped
closer and touched her cheek. When she turned to him
in surprise, he took advantage and brushed a soft kiss
across her lips. She started to say something, but he put
a finger across the lips he'd just touched with his own.

Then he smiled. "That wasn't a real kiss, either."

NOT A REAL KISS. Olivia couldn't believe she'd let Alex
have the last word—again. The fact irked her through
the cardboard-tasting dinner she'd choked down while
she stood at the kitchen counter, through the brief,
frigid trip to the high school gymnasium, through the
typically frenetic pace of the basketball game. Now,
having said good-night to the children and left the outside light on for Wolf, who had a date, she shut herself
inside her bedroom and sat down on the bed to take off
her boots.

Not a real kiss. Then what on earth was it? The ini-
tial step of seduction? He'd already pulled that in the
Ferrari last week, but his closeness hadn't resulted in a

kiss, although it wouldn't have taken much for that to ·
happen. She'd been too willing—a fact that she found
embarrassing, now that she'd had time to think about
it. She should have known better, of course. Alexander Leeds was what her mother would call a playboy
but she was no gullible young woman with a head full
of romantic fantasies. She was a practical mother, for
heaven's sake.

Maybe she should have asked him to the basketball
game. Was that what he'd wanted? It would have served
him right to have to sit on hard wooden bleachers amid
screaming teenagers and excited parents.

And what did she, Olivia Bennett, mother of three,
want? Certainly not another "relationship." Oh, how
she hated that word! Especially not one with Doomed
to Fail written all over it. She wasn't stupid.

Tempted, but not stupid.

Olivia was too tired to worry about Alex anymore.
She stripped off her jeans and sweatshirt and tossed
them onto the floor of her closet. When she opened her
dresser drawer, she pulled out a very practical flannel
nightgown. She frowned at the jumble of flannel inside the drawer. Actually, she could close her eyes, se-
lect any nightgown, and it would scream back at her
"Practical single mother living alone, with absolutely
no sex life!" She frowned and opened the next drawer.
Its contents weren't any better—just a mixture of cotton briefs and basic brassieres. No scraps of satin and
lace peeked from any corner.

No-frills underwear for a no-frills woman? Olivia
slammed the drawers shut and turned away, disgusted
by the evidence of her practicality.

She tossed the soft gown over her naked body and buttoned the bodice. The body wasn't in bad shape. She still had curves in the right place, and sit-ups had kept her stomach taut even after having given birth to three children. Not bad for thirty-six.

Oh, well, at least she wore interesting earrings. And Alexander Leeds—no matter how sexy and charming—was the man who would see that Fancy Nancy or Glitter Girl or whatever he wanted to call it would make a lot of money.

Someday soon she'd be able to buy as many pairs of silk underwear as she wanted. Whether or not anyone but herself ever saw them.

4

"I DON'T ATTEND children's birthday parties." This wasn't the first time Alex had uttered those words, but Olivia continued to remain oblivious to his reluctance.

"Why not? It's not such a big deal." She sprinkled little candy things onto the pink frosted tops of cupcakes. "The girls will come here after school, eat cake and ice cream, Nancy will open her presents, and after they make earrings they'll go home. We're talking three hours, max."

"Easy for you to say." Alex was cornered and struggled for a way to get out of the bind he was in. "I told you, I'm not good with children."

Olivia didn't look surprised. "So?"

"I have to experi—"

"What about Weepy Wilma?"

He hated it when she interrupted him. Especially when she backed him into a corner like this. "I hired a research firm, of course."

"Well, since we don't have the money for research firms, we do our own." She arranged the cupcakes on a foil-covered plate, then looked up with a reassuring smile. "Don't think of it as a birthday party—think of it as firsthand experience with the product."

What he'd like would be some firsthand experience with the product's inventor, but Alex didn't say so. He wished she hadn't braided her hair this afternoon. She looked too proper, though there was nothing proper in the way her white sweater fitted her curvy little body. He could think of better things to do today than watch children paint earrings. "Did I tell you I found a glue supplier?"

"Within budget?"

He nodded. "Of course." He'd had a busy week. Two other campaigns had needed attention, then he'd had several meetings with food brokers in Boston and New York about a new line of salad dressings. He'd planned on spending this Friday catching up on paperwork, followed by a date with a leggy brunette model he'd met Wednesday on the New York shuttle.

That is, until Olivia called him, reminding him about the earring party. He'd been forced to make some slight adjustments in his workday, although he still planned to pick up Jill at eight. All of his attempts to date Olivia had failed. He told himself that he wasn't giving up, not really, but would step back and continue with his normal life, just as he would have if he'd never met her.

Still, that was easier said than done.

"I've packed the kits according to the specifications we outlined last week." She moved to the sink and washed the frosting from her hands.

"Into what?" They hadn't selected packing yet.

"Ice cube trays." She grinned at him. "Stroke of genius, huh? Let me show you."

Alex followed her to the basement and noticed that more card tables had been set up, flanked with an odd assortment of folding chairs. "How many girls are coming over here today?"

"Ten, including Nancy."

Alex gulped. He approached the tables, where neat rows of plastic ice cube trays sat. Each compartment held glitter, plastic "jewels" or earrings. "Very nice," he murmured. "I'm impressed."

"Think these would work with the kit?"

"It's possible," he said, picking up one of the trays. "It certainly deserves some thought."

Was that a compliment? Olivia didn't know if she heard him correctly. Alex certainly didn't give out compliments easily, unless they were alone in a man-woman situation. And she was determined to avoid those kinds of encounters, especially today, when Alex, in baggy cotton slacks and multicolored sweater, looked gorgeous. The brown triangles matched his eyes. She had no doubt that he'd picked the sweater precisely for that reason.

He turned those brown eyes upon her. "Where are the boys? Do they usually help with these things?"

"No way. Wolf has practice, Josh is at a friend's house, and Nancy is upstairs in her room, trying on outfits for today."

"Then we're alone."

"In a way, I guess." She stepped away from the table.

"That doesn't happen very often. Not since we went up to the mall."

"That was business."

"Forget business for a minute, Olivia. Are you free for dinner next week?"

Olivia yearned to say yes, but common sense stopped her. "I really don't think that would be a good idea."

"Too bad. I was hoping you'd change your mind about going out with me."

"You know I'm not your type."

"Have I ever said that?"

His lopsided grin made her think he hadn't been serious about the question. She shrugged, pretending indifference. "Not in so many words, but . . ."

Alex returned the tray to the table and studied Olivia's expression as if he wondered what she was really thinking. "Then how do you know?"

"Just a feeling." She edged away. She had no intention of getting involved in such a silly discussion when she had so much work to do before the guests arrived. "Look, I really have to get back upstairs now."

"Do you have more to do for this party or are you avoiding me?"

"Both," she admitted. "I'm not used to being flirted with."

His eyebrows rose. "No?"

"Except for you, that is."

"If it will make it easier for you, I promise not to say a word to you that isn't professional and business-orientated. And I can quite easily take your word for the market research and leave. Right now, in fact."

"Forget it, Alex. You're not going anywhere."

He sighed and shoved his hands into his pockets. "I was afraid you'd say something like that. I suppose you want me to set the dining room table with little pink paper plates?"

"Yellow plates." Olivia felt oddly unsettled. One minute he was asking her to go out with him, the next he was begging to leave the house. She didn't understand him—or maybe it was the entire male species she didn't comprehend.

He followed her back upstairs. Within the hour the party was in full swing, a guaranteed success the minute Nancy's friends saw the balloons and potato chips. Alex attempted to remain in the background, leaning against the dining room wall, well out of the way. He watched Olivia laugh with the children and regretted her refusal to date him. Well, he decided, he'd given it another shot. He'd back off and date the model, prowl through the health club next week, and maybe even plan a skiing weekend in New Hampshire.

He'd forget this strange attraction to Olivia, domestic goddess and reluctant business associate. Forget that she took his breath away whenever she walked into a room. Forget the sweet taste of those soft lips and the delicate tremor just beneath her skin whenever he touched her.

He'd also have to forget his plans to get to know her, kiss her, make love to her. The lady wasn't willing, didn't have the time, and remained totally oblivious to his attentions.

That in itself was cause for worry.

IF SHE CAUGHT ALEX looking at his watch again, Olivia knew she'd strike him with the pizza slicer. It was a heavy, commercial slicer, too, and would probably pack quite a wallop, especially if she aimed it correctly. Melted cheese and sticky sauce would drip red streaks onto that expensive sweater. The blood would stain.

Olivia shook her head. She'd watched too many action movies with the boys this year.

The party started with lots of giggles, then Olivia brought out the pizzas she'd constructed this morning before work. Once the last pizza had been cooked and eaten, it would be time to sing "Happy Birthday" and blow out the candles on the cupcakes.

She had swallowed her first bite of pizza when the phone rang. A few minutes later she returned to the dining room and approached Alex. "I have to pick up Wolf. Can you finish up the dessert with the girls?"

"I'll go get him," he offered, putting his empty paper plate upon the table. "Where is he?"

"Thanks, but I have to go myself. His coach wants to talk to me about something, he said. I won't be long." She beckoned Nancy over. "You can open your presents now. Mr. Leeds will be here with you—I have to get Wolf."

Nancy's slice of pizza halted in midair. "I thought he got a ride home with Becky."

"Guess not. I need to go to the high school. I'll be back soon."

"What about the earring party?"

"Mr. Leeds will help—and you know more about making earrings than anybody. You show him how to do it, okay? And he'll help the rest of the kids."

Nancy didn't look convinced. "He's a boy. I didn't want, you know, *boys* at my party."

"Sorry, hon. It can't be helped."

Alex chuckled at Nancy's disappointed expression. He didn't get extra points with either of the Bennett women. "I promise—cross my heart—that I'll stay out of the way."

"Well . . ."

Olivia tried again. "I'll light the candles and watch you blow them out, all right?"

Nancy smiled at her mother. "Okay. Just don't forget the camera this time."

Olivia lighted the candles and deposited the platter of cupcakes in front of Nancy while everyone sang the "Happy Birthday" song. She grabbed the camera from its place on top of the refrigerator and told Nancy to smile. Olivia snapped several pictures, then handed the small camera to Alex. "Would you take some pictures of the presents being opened? And if I'm not back before they go downstairs, would you take some of them making earrings?"

"No problem." At least he could handle that, he knew. The rest of this filled him with dread. His stomach lurched as Olivia opened the hall door and shrugged on her winter coat. He was responsible for ten little girls? *Ten!* He was being punished for something he'd done in the past. He only wished he knew exactly what—and hoped he'd enjoyed himself.

"Can we have some more soda?" one of the girls asked, holding out a paper cup.

Alex looked at Nancy, who waved toward the kitchen. "There's lots more in the refrigerator."

He went into the narrow galley kitchen and approached the refrigerator. It had an amazing door, covered with various notes, messages, a grocery list, birthday cards and family photographs. He was lucky he could find the handle. He opened the door, and the sight of large plastic bottles of soda greeted him. He picked out diet cola and root beer to bring back to the thirsty children. He started to set one upon the counter, but there wasn't a clear spot to be seen. The white Formica was covered with pizza pans and rumpled yellow napkins. A glob of pizza sauce slid off the edge of the counter and attached itself to his hip.

Alex tried to wipe the spot with a napkin, but it only grew worse.

Nancy appeared at his side. "Can't you find the soda?"

"I was just bringing it in." He tossed the stained napkin onto the counter to join the rest of the trash and reached for the bottles. "These okay?"

"Sure."

Alex started to follow Nancy into the dining room, but she stopped. "What about the ice cream?"

"I have to do ice cream?"

She looked at him as if he was crazy. "Sure. It's a birthday party—there's always ice cream."

"I didn't know." His childhood birthday parties had been limited to uncomfortable restaurant dinners with his father. And his adult birthdays had been hardly thought of; there'd been a few years when he'd altogether forgotten the date had come and gone.

"Don't you ever go to parties?"

"Yeah, I go to parties."

"What about your birthday?"

Alex handed the child the bottles of soda. He opened the freezer and found two half gallons of ice cream in front of him. "What about it?"

Nancy sighed. "When is it?"

"In February."

"That's not far away."

"Guess not." He shoved the mess on the counter toward the sink and put down the icy cartons. "Do I scoop from here or out there?"

"Out there. We get to pick."

"Right." Naturally it wouldn't be easy.

"The scoop is in that drawer." She pointed to a narrow drawer three inches to the left of his pizza sauce stain. Sure enough, he rifled through it and found an ice-cream scoop. "Your mom sure has a lot of utensils."

When he turned back, Nancy was gone. With the soda. He looked through the doorway and saw her twisting the top off the root beer. He piled one carton on top of the other and carried them into the dining room. "Who wants, uh, chocolate chip and who wants cherry crunch?"

He negotiated the girls' demands and managed not to spill anything on them or himself. The girls ate cheerfully, with surprisingly good manners and enthusiastic conversations about school, music and movies. They were actually very civilized, Alex noted, as he shoved the remainder of the ice cream back into the freezer compartment. When he returned to the dining room, the party was breaking up.

"We're ready to make earrings now, Uncle Alex," Nancy announced.

Uncle Alex? Alex cleared his throat. "Great. Go down and get started and I'll clean up here."

"That's okay. We'll do it," she said, and grabbed the wastebasket from the corner. Minutes later the girls had cleaned up the mess. "I'll open my presents when Mom comes back, Uncle Alex."

She'd said it again. Alex bent down and whispered, "What's with the 'Uncle Alex' stuff?"

Nancy looked behind her, as if checking that none of her friends was close by and whispered, "That's what my friends call their mothers' boyfriends. I couldn't call you Mr. Leeds. I'd sound like a geek."

"But I'm not your mother's boyfriend."

"*They* don't know that."

"I see your point." He straightened. "All right, I'll go along with it, just for today."

"Thanks." Her smile almost knocked him over. Those blue eyes lighted up just like her mother's.

"No problem. Just do me a favor and keep the nail polish away from me. These are new clothes."

"Too late, Uncle Alex. I think those pants are *destroyed*."

He grimaced. "Don't say that. You wouldn't believe how much they cost."

"Mom has stain remover stuff. You want me to get it for you?"

"Don't worry about it." He looked at his watch. Olivia had only been gone for twenty minutes. Surely she couldn't still be talking to the basketball coach? She would have to be on her way home soon; the high school was only ten minutes away.

Alex decided the dining room looked as good as it was going to for a while. The girlish shrieks from the basement made him long to stay upstairs and hide, but he'd promised Olivia he would supervise.

And he really did want to see how the earring kits worked. He took the camera with him. Pictures of the process would come in handy, convincing buyers of the enjoyment children would derive from the product.

Strictly business, he assured himself. And not because he wanted to impress Olivia with his ability to step in and handle problems on a minute's notice. Although, he decided, heading toward the open basement door, she'd have to realize he'd done an extraordinary job.

Scooping ice cream was easier than making earrings. He pried off the stubborn lids of nail polish containers, his only reward a shy thanks, and inhaled the overpowering smell of chemicals without passing out. He was careful not to drip onto his clothes and to avoid the tiny brushes that the girls held and swooped and carefully refilled.

"Here, Uncle Alex. You try." Nancy handed him a bottle of blue polish and couple of metal flowers.

He handed it back to her. "I'm just supervising, thanks."

Nancy's brow wrinkled. "Don't you want to?"

Alex felt like a jerk. He'd probably ruin her party if he didn't participate. He forced a smile, took the earrings and the bottle, and sat down on a metal chair between Nancy and a serious little redhead.

When Nancy told him to paint, he painted. While waiting for one to dry, he painted another. Then he glued, dipped into gold glitter, and set his creations to dry on the inverted egg cartons. The girls didn't seem to have any problems with the process. They remained fascinated by the various colors of nail polish available; selecting the beads and stones to use took longer and caused more discussions than Alex would ever have thought possible.

"What about the green ones?" the little redhead asked. "Do you think they go with the black paint?"

It took Alex a minute to realize she was talking to him. He looked at the green "gems" in her palm. "I suppose so."

"Or the pearls?"

"Pearls are always appropriate," he answered, keeping his expression bland.

"I'm using gold glitter."

A thick layer of glitter lay plastered on heart-shaped earrings. "I see that. Then the pearls might be a little too much." He obediently looked into the tray she held out for his inspection. "What about the blue?"

Nancy leaned over his shoulder to look. "Black and blue? No way, Audrey."

Audrey smiled at Alex and took back her tray. "I like the green."

"Excellent choice," he muttered. "Maybe I should go clean up the kitchen."

Nancy looked pointedly at the camera. "What about the pictures?"

"Oh, that's right. I forgot." He took a few snapshots of the girls at the long table, then some close-ups of the more successful versions of the earrings. He'd thought the earrings in the gift shops gaudy—these looked wild. At least most of them did. Some were actually very neat, showing that the girls took their work very seriously. He turned back to sit down at the table once again—and knocked over the bottle of cola, right into his crotch. It spread down one thigh, took a sharp left and rolled onto the floor. Alex sat frozen for a moment.

Nancy shook her head. "You'd better throw those pants away. You're having bad luck today."

"I'll just clean up, thanks," he said, looking for a paper towel or a napkin to wipe up the spill.

Nancy rushed out of the room and returned with a roll of paper towels. "Here."

"Thanks."

"Can you wash them?"

"I will later." He couldn't believe how much of a mess he was in. Maybe washing the pants wasn't such a bad idea.

"I can get you a pair of sweatpants."

"Great." Wolf's pants would be a little long, but with sweats it wouldn't matter. "I'll just go get out of these."

Alex hurried upstairs and into the bathroom off the hall. He removed his pants, found a washcloth in the cupboard and wet it with warm water. Then he attempted to clean the sticky cola from his bare legs. Even his briefs were wet. He might as well have sat in the soda for the mess it had made.

"Here," Nancy said from outside. Alex opened the door a crack and she shoved a pair of pants through the opening. He took one look at them and froze. "Nancy, wait—"

But it was too late. He could already hear her thudding downstairs. The pants were not Wolf's but Olivia's. Lavender knit.

He'd have to stretch his sweater over his hips or he'd scare the girls. Maybe. They didn't look as if they'd scare too easily. When he finally went downstairs, they were still immersed in their earrings. No one said a word about his pants.

Alex sat down beside Nancy and whispered, "Didn't Wolf have any sweatpants I could have borrowed?"

Nancy looked shocked. "I'm not allowed to go in his room. He'd kill me."

She was probably right. He could feel that particular urge himself.

"Can you put the hooks on?" a little girl asked.

With some instruction from Nancy he was able to help assemble the finished products; the girls lined up or passed him the earrings.

"How's it going?"

"Mom!" Nancy cried, lifting an earring from a bowl of silver glitter. "I saved my presents for you."

"Is everyone having fun?" Olivia asked, looking at Alex, who sat with a pile of earring hooks in front of him.

"Uncle Alex is getting the hang of it," Nancy assured her.

"Maybe Mr. Leeds would like a break."

"Yes." Mr. Leeds wanted a drink. *Make that a double.* His head had been pounding for the past fifteen minutes, and he realized he needed aspirin more than alcohol. He started to stand up, but remembered just in time that he was wearing lavender pants, so sat down again. "What took you so long?"

"What an afternoon!" Olivia pulled over an empty chair and sat down, too.

"What happened?" Alex suddenly realized how tired Olivia looked. Her skin was a milky white, highlighted only by two spots of red on her cheeks.

"The battery went dead."

"Did you have to jump it?"

She nodded. "It took a while to hunt down the janitor and find someone who had jumper cables we could borrow. Brad—that's the coach—had a truck but no cables."

He wondered how well she knew the coach. He'd never thought too much about her social life. Maybe he had better assess the competition and see what he was up against. That is, if he really wanted to compete for Mother Goose's attention. "What did, uh, Brad have to say?"

She shot him an odd look. "Oh, it was about Wolf and a possible basketball scholarship. There are some papers I need to fill out, just in case he qualifies for one."

"And does he?"

"Maybe. We'll have to wait and see." She looked around at the earrings that were being created. "How is everything going here?"

"Fine," Alex answered. "Just perfect."

"I knew you could do it," she said, clearly missing the sarcasm. "It wasn't too bad, was it?"

Only when compared to a root canal, but he wouldn't let her know that. He'd like to see the Coach handle a pair of needle-nosed pliers and ten glitter-dusted females. "No."

"Do you see what I mean now, about how this keeps children busy?"

"Yes."

"And it's fun at the same time. And creative."

"Yes."

"And they can wear them, actually have something to use when they're done."

"True." He tried to make himself heard above the happy chatter. "Could I have a couple of aspirin?"

"Of course." She frowned. "The smell is pretty bad in here. You should have opened the windows and turned on the fans." She did those things herself, then beckoned Alex toward the stairs. "How about a cup of coffee?"

"I don't think so. Just the aspirin will be fine."

"Call me if you need me," she told Nancy. "I'll only be a minute."

"Can I open my presents now?"

"Why don't you wait until everyone is finished with the earrings? They don't have to rush, and can take their trays home with them. They don't have to make them all at once."

A chorus of cheers filled the room. He waited for Olivia to turn away before he rose from his seat. Alex wondered if he'd ever get his aspirin; it seemed as though the rest of the birthday party would be following him upstairs.

Wolf leaned against the kitchen counter, half a cupcake in his hand. Alex was grateful for the sight of another male.

"Hey," Wolf said.

Alex accepted the greeting. "How you doin'?"

Wolf nodded, his mouth full. He swallowed, and Alex watched his Adam's apple bob down and up. "Okay. You?"

"Not bad." *I'm just covered with glitter, have a migraine headache, and am wearing women's pants.*

Olivia came out of the kitchen with a glass of water and the aspirin bottle. "Here, Alex. I hope this helps."

Wolf grinned. "I heard you got stuck with the party animals."

Olivia stopped short. "Why are you wearing my sweatpants?"

He ignored the question, took the bottle, poured out two pills, then took the water Olivia held out to him. "Thanks." After he'd swallowed the aspirin, he winced. "It's a long story, involving a bottle of soda. I guess the nail polish smell got to me."

"I appreciated the help," Olivia said softly. "But where are your pants?"

"In the bathroom. Nancy wanted to wash them, but I stalled her. Well," he said, moving toward the door. "I hope you get a new battery—"

They were interrupted by the sound of feet pounding on the stairs. "Time for the presents!" Nancy called. "Remember?"

Wolf slid towards the living room. "Exit time."

Olivia looked at her watch. "Perfect timing. The mothers will be here in about ten minutes."

Alex heard the tiredness in her voice, despite her efforts to hide it. Again he noted her pale skin and the faint smudge of dark circles under those glorious blue eyes. "Rough week?"

"It's tax season."

"Judd's working you too hard."

"It's not Judd—it's everything. It's a rough time of year, and I have too many things to keep me busy."

Meaning too many things to worry about. "Let me worry about the business."

"All right, maybe I will." Olivia pushed her hair away from her forehead. "And I'll let Judd worry about taxes and I'll worry about everything else."

"Which is?"

"Money, kids, bills, school, and cars that won't start."

"Wolf can put a battery in the Buick, can't he?"

"I'll ask him. Maybe I don't even need a new battery."

"You will. This is the first sign."

"It is?"

"Trust me."

"The last man who said 'Trust me' tried to sell me a condominium."

"Well, trust me, anyway. You're going to need a battery, unless the one you have now is new."

Olivia thought for a minute. "No, it's not." She chuckled. "There's not a damn thing around this house that's new."

"Except me."

She chuckled again. He was glad to see her smile. "That's true."

"And there are dozens of new earrings downstairs."

"Weren't they awful?"

"Awful," he agreed.

"But you can see how it works, can't you?"

"I see. It sure kept them busy."

"Why did Nancy call you Uncle Alex?"

"She said all he friends call their mother's boyfriends 'Uncle.' She didn't want to look odd."

"*She* didn't want to look odd?" Olivia laughed. "You might want to leave before the mothers come."

"That's the best idea I've heard all day."

5

ALEX HURRIED TO HIS CAR, hoping none of Olivia's neighbors would notice the purple pants sticking out under his trench coat. He drove quickly, the ten minutes to his home in Wakefield uncomplicated by the light swirls of snowflakes beginning to dust the windshield.

He'd chosen the twelve-room Victorian for its huge barn of a garage. Behind the small town of Wakefield, in an area of older homes and oak trees, Alex's house occupied a large corner lot. With its white clapboard and Newport-blue trim, it looked like anything but a bachelor retreat. Alex loved it.

Once he'd parked the car in the garage and entered the house, he paid no further attention to his surroundings, except to appreciate the sudden silence. He inhaled deeply. No shrieking little girls, no complaints or giggles. No dripping ice cream or spattered fingernail polish. He was home, in pristine silence and blessed isolation.

Alex headed directly upstairs to the largest bedroom at the end of the hall. Not a moment too soon, as far as he was concerned; the right side of his head throbbed with a deep pain that, despite the aspirin he'd already taken, showed no signs of leaving.

He went into the bathroom and stripped quickly, dropping the dirty clothes into a hamper where the cleaning lady would deal with them Monday morning. He turned on the shower and stepped beneath it, making certain the hot spray didn't hit the pounding side of his head. Long minutes passed while he stood there and let the heat penetrate his chilled and sticky skin.

He'd almost felt guilty leaving Olivia to ten or more children and a messy house. But this afternoon had proved he had been right all along. Her life was full of basketball games and children. Their relationship—if there ever were to be one—would have to be squeezed in between basketball games and Scout meetings. He would always come in fourth.

And he wasn't used to that.

"I'm a selfish bastard," he mumbled, stepping out of the shower. He wrapped a white towel around his waist and decided against bending over to dry any more of his body. His head might fall right off his shoulders if he did.

He sat down carefully on the bed and reached for the phone, punching out the numbers swiftly, hoping to catch Paula before she left for the weekend.

"Leeds. Good afternoon."

"Hello, Paula. Just thought I'd see if there were any messages that couldn't wait until Monday morning."

"There aren't. The people from Baby Love want a meeting and Mr. Docker, the man with that strange soap dish, wanted to know if you'd heard anything from Sears yet. I told them you'd talk to them Monday morning. How was the earring party?"

"Educational."

She chuckled. "I'll bet."

"Careful, or you may have to go to the next one."

"My granddaughter would love it. Anything else you need me to do before I lock up?"

"Yes," he said, making a quick decision. "Call the Sheraton—the one by the airport—and make my apologies to Jill Patterson about this evening."

"What should I tell her?"

"The truth. That I've been taken ill."

"Another migraine, huh?" Her voice was sympathetic.

"Yes," he answered, closing his eyes. "And it's called Glitter Girl."

"Oh, those fancy earrings shouldn't give you any trouble. I thought you were coming to enjoy that account...."

Alex could still smell nail polish. "It's not the account, it's the market research."

"Well, whatever it is, I gave those earrings you gave me to my ten-year-old granddaughter, and she was thrilled. Maybe you could invite us to the next earring party."

"I promise. If I survive tonight."

"What else do you want me to do? You sound like you need to be in bed."

"Just send the flowers to Jill—anything but roses, but nothing cheap. Say something clever. I can't think of anything right now."

"You just go to bed, Alex."

"Thanks, Paula. Have a good weekend."

"You, too. Take good care of yourself. You know how you overdo."

"I'll be fine," Alex promised. He hung up the receiver and switched the dial to Off. He didn't bother turning on the answering machine; he wouldn't return any calls tonight, anyway. Then he grabbed an ice bag from the bathroom cupboard and padded downstairs to the kitchen for ice. That accomplished, he returned to his bathroom and rummaged through the medicine cabinet until he found the medication the doctor had prescribed for migraines. He swallowed two red capsules and said a quick prayer for relief.

He turned up the heat on the bedroom thermostat, dropped the damp towel to the floor and slid between the crisp white sheets. He stretched under the king-size navy quilt that covered the water bed and held the plump bag to the side of his head. He closed his eyes and breathed deeply. The silence was heaven, especially after the hell of the afternoon.

Actually, it really hadn't been that bad. He'd survived. Barely. To look at him, anyone would think he'd been devastated by ten girls and a few bottle of nail polish. It was the smell, he decided. The fumes had made him crazy, ruined his depth perception and triggered a migraine.

He thought of Olivia. No, he didn't want to think of Olivia. She'd looked exhausted and been unwilling to admit it. Damn, he liked the looks of that woman. Just the sight of her turned him on, made him want to carry her off to a room with no doors and windows and make love to her for a few days or weeks. No interruptions. He'd like to see what that lovely body promised. He'd like to be looking into those soft blue eyes when he entered her, hard and sure. She'd be warm, and he—

Damn. She'd probably eat some of that horrible pizza for dinner and then head out to the ball game in a car that was only fit for a demolition derby. He worried about her. Which was perfectly normal in a consultant-client relationship, he assured himself.

Alex struggled to sit up, letting the ice bag fall to land beside his hip. He reached for the phone once again, muttered an oath and dialed. She wouldn't go out with him, but she sure as hell would have to accept some help. That is, if he had any say in it.

POLLY TURNED from the door to call to her friend. "Did you order dinner, Olivia? What a good idea!"

"I didn't order anything." Olivia looked past Polly; an unfamiliar teenager stood on the front step. He handed her friend a large brown paper bag and turned away. Polly shut the door and walked across the living room. She set the bag upon the dining room table and peered inside. "Maybe Wolf did."

Olivia put down a sponge and came out of the kitchen. "I doubt it. He just left—Becky picked him up for the game tonight."

"Well, whoever ordered had good taste," Polly said, lifting a white carton from the bag. "I hope you're hungry. This is from Sea View, that Chinese restaurant that specializes in spicy seafood."

Olivia inhaled. "It smells wonderful. Do you think they delivered to the wrong house?"

"It's possible," Polly said, returning the carton to the bag and neatly folding the top.

"I'll call them and find out. I'd hate to think that someone else down the street was waiting for their dinner to arrive." She went into the kitchen. A few minutes later she had her answer. When she came back into the dining room, Polly sat at the table eating the last cupcake. The sounds of Paula Abdul pounded faintly from down the hall. Nancy and her best friend—Polly's daughter, Jen—were closeted in Nancy's bedroom, practicing dance routines.

Olivia sat down and peered into the bag. Her mouth watered. "There wasn't any mistake."

"Then who ordered it?"

"It was sent by Alexander Leeds."

Polly stopped chewing and stared. She finally swallowed and set the half-eaten cake upon the table. "Why?"

"I don't know."

"Call him and find out."

"I hope he doesn't plan on coming back here to eat this with me."

Polly shrugged. "So what? There's enough food in this bag for six people."

Olivia looked inside the bag a second time and saw the white cartons neatly stacked inside. "You're right. I wonder what's going on."

"Maybe he was thinking of the kids."

"Alexander? Don't be funny. He hardly knows what children are." Olivia frowned at the bag. "I wonder what's in there. I'm really hungry—that pizza was terrible."

"So? Eat."

Olivia didn't have to think about it any longer. "Want to join me?"

Polly looked at her watch. "Sure. But I'll get the plates," she ordered, standing up. "You look wiped out. I'm going to tell Judd that he has to ease up."

Olivia chuckled and sat down at the table. "He can't. It's tax season." When Polly returned with plates and flatware, Olivia added, "Besides, it's not Judd's fault. I'm working on the earring business, too, which takes up the rest of my time. Which is my choice."

"Okay, okay. I won't bother Judd, if you promise to take care of yourself." Polly opened a container. "It's our lucky day—lemon shrimp."

Olivia reached inside the bag and pulled out another box. "Garlic something—I can smell it before I open it."

"Yum—here's white rice, chopsticks and lots of those sauce packets."

They lined up the boxes on the table, finding batter-fried shrimp, spicy eggplant and something Polly identified as Hunan scallops.

"Obviously Alex knows you like Chinese food."

"He *assumed* I liked Chinese food."

"And do you?"

"I used to. Actually, I haven't eaten it in years."

Polly made a face at her friend. "You haven't *dated* in years, either."

"Be nice. I went out with that accountant last year."

"True. He wanted to take you to Florida."

"Correction. He wanted to take me to bed."

"Okay. That, too." Polly put down her chopsticks and eyed Olivia. "The big question is, what does Alexander Leeds want?"

"Maybe the same thing." Olivia stabbed a lemon shrimp with her fork. "Instead, he's going to get my thanks for the food."

"You think that's all he wants—to get you into bed? Surprise, surprise. You two looked quite cozy at my party. And now you're working together. Physical attraction is inevitable. You're both attractive, single—"

"Stop." Olivia didn't know how to explain. "I'm not saying I'm not attracted to him, but it's not that simple. The man baffles me. One minute he's asking me out, the next he's trying to get out of helping with the earring party. Then he manages to keep the girls occupied—but walks out of the house in my sweatpants."

Polly smiled. "I heard about the accident. Jen couldn't wait to tell me. He must have been furious."

"Actually, I don't think he was."

Polly scraped the final spoonful of vegetables out of the eggplant carton. "Guess not—he sent you a great present."

"But why?"

"He likes you."

Olivia shook her head. "You were right before. He wants something."

Polly shrugged and suggested, "Maybe he was just being nice."

Olivia shrugged back. "We'll see. Whatever his reasons, the food is delicious."

"Are you going to call him?"

Olivia looked at her watch. "I'll wait. Are you sure you want Nancy to sleep over?"

"Of course I do. We've rented some movies, bought soda and a new box of microwave popcorn. Judd's working late, so they'll have the family room all to themselves. What else could two girls want?"

"Josh is at a friend's house, too."

"Will you be lonesome?"

"No. I'm going to bed early for once. I would have gone to the game, but I'm afraid I'll get stuck again with that car. Alex said I need a new battery, so I guess I'll

have to make an appointment at the garage this weekend."

"Well, call Judd if you need a ride to work Monday."
Polly stood and started gathering up the plates. "Now
I'm going to help you clean this place up."

"You don't—"

"Yes, I want to. You look like you're ready to drop
onto the floor."

Olivia studied herself in the mirror when she was
washing up before bed. Polly had been right. She did
look tired. She patted her skin dry with a towel, then
brushed her hair. It was getting long—time for a trim,
if she could find half an hour for a trip to the hairdres-
ser's. She sat down on the bed, kicked off her slippers
and slid under the flowered comforter. The pattern of
the new sheet she'd bought matched the floral print of
the fluffy blanket. Olivia loved her bedroom. After Jack
had left, she'd done it over the way she'd always wanted
to. Sheer, gathered lace curtains hung from the tops of
the double-hung windows, and several embroidered
pictures she'd found in her mother's belongings were
now framed and hung on the plain white walls. It was
a woman's bedroom, right down to the round table beside the bed, with its Victorian lace toppings and the
antique-framed picture of Olivia's parents. The children had given her a crystal bird for Christmas, and it
rested between a blue lamp and the telephone.

There wasn't a masculine thing in the room.

The realization gave her no comfort. She'd liked being married, had loved the warmth beside her at night,
enjoyed the crisp look of a man's white shirts hanging
in the closet and in the sight of yesterday's folded
newspaper on the nightstand. And, of course, there had

been the "penny bowl"—that ceramic saucer into which Jack had emptied his pockets each evening.

Yes, she'd liked being married. But she didn't know if she could do it again, wasn't certain if she could ever risk her nicely repaired heart for the sake of a warm body next to hers in bed and a convenient container of change.

Olivia wondered what Alex's bedroom looked like. She pictured modern black and white or a collage of neutrals. And something glass filled with change on a sleek black bureau. He had probably never considered marriage, never yearned for floral comforters on his bed or pink slippers on the carpet.

Alex. Olivia smiled as she reached for the lamp's switch. She'd have to call him, even if she only had his office number. She promised herself she'd leave a message to thank him. And the next time she saw him, she'd have to ask him why he'd sent such a thoughtful and surprising gift.

"IT'S THE WAY to a woman's heart," Alex teased. "Haven't you heard that expression before?"

"Yes," Olivia said. "But I thought it only applied to men."

"Wrong again," he said. His brown eyes twinkled at her and he looked very much as if he was going to step closer for a kiss, "real" or not.

"Thank you. It was very thoughtful—and very good, too." Olivia took a step back, suddenly realizing she shouldn't have broached the subject while they were alone together in the basement. The kids had finished their chores and their earring work for the day. She'd never expected Alex to show up Saturday at noon and ask if there were any leftovers from the Sea View.

"You're welcome," he replied, looking amused.

Olivia hurried to change the subject. "I didn't think you'd be coming here today, although I'm glad you did. We need to go over the presentation for the bank."

"Give me what you've done so far and I'll take it home with me."

"I told the loan officer I'd give her the application first thing Monday morning."

"No problem," he assured her. "I'll give it back to you tomorrow. But that's not why I came here today."

"This is business."

Alex grinned. "It's the only way I get to see you. And besides, it wasn't business the night we met."

Olivia hesitated. She'd had too many daydreams about the evening they'd met—a magical Christmas evening with candles and twinkling tree lights and golden champagne. He'd worn an expensive suit and his tie, when she'd looked closely, had had a pattern of minuscule holly leaves on a charcoal background. "No, but . . ."

"We could start over," Alex suggested, his voice soft. He touched her hair. "You have glitter in your hair."

"An occupational hazard."

"We started something that evening," he said. "Why won't you go out with me?"

"It wouldn't work." *Because you're too handsome, too charming and much too sexy,* she wanted to say, but didn't intend to fuel his ego any further.

"How do you know without ever giving it a chance?"

Olivia shook her head. "I don't mind dating once in a while, Alex, but I'm not, I mean, I just don't go around having affairs. It's not my style." She could feel the heat on her face.

"Your style is home-cooked meals and picnics with the kids, right?"

"You make that sound awful."

"I don't mean to, except that you're forgetting you're a warm, sexy, desirable woman."

Olivia opened her mouth to protest, but he'd stepped close to her and touched her lips with his. His mouth felt wonderful. His lips were warm, the gentle pressure increasing until he grasped her shoulders and held her. Olivia wouldn't have moved, anyway. The kiss was altogether too satisfying, too enjoyable to stop. He lifted his mouth for a second, then he slowly slanted his lips across hers again. This time he made the kiss last, taking his time, although still not urging Olivia's lips to part. When he released her mouth, he loosened his grip on her shoulders and waited.

"Well?" he asked finally.

"I'm not forgetting anything," she replied, keeping her voice soft. "I simply choose not to get . . . involved with any one right now, not at this time of my life."

He frowned. "Not involved with anyone or not involved with *me*?"

She looked away, which gave him the answer he needed. "I'd better heat up those leftovers," she said, stepping away from him now. "Did you want some?"

"Sure," he muttered. "But I came here to work."

She looked back over her shoulder, surprise written all over her lovely face. "Work?"

"I came to help. Teach me to do something." He grinned. "I even wore old clothes."

Olivia doubted the snug jeans and blue sweatshirt were old. The man wouldn't condescend to look anything but his best, no matter what. She was absolutely positive he owned more clothes than she did—more than her entire family put together, for that matter. "All right. First we'll have lunch, then you can paint findings, and then we'll do inventory. I need to place another order for supplies."

He didn't hesitate. "I think I can handle that."

That was the trouble, Olivia knew, heading upstairs with Alex following close behind. The man figured he could handle anything.

"Is Wolf around?" he asked when they reached the hall. "I'm going to need his help with something."

"He was taking a shower the last time I was up here." Olivia called up the stairway. "Wolf?"

"Yeah?"

"Alex needs to talk to you."

"Alex can eat first," he said from beside her. "No hurry," he called. There was no answer, so Alex followed Olivia into the kitchen and watched as she opened the refrigerator. "What's left?"

"Some of the eggplant and the batter-fried shrimp. Polly was here last night and we shared."

"Who won the basketball game?"

"The other team. I didn't go. Wolf got a ride with his girlfriend because I didn't want to risk using the car again." She emptied the cartons into saucepans and put them on the stove to heat.

"That's another reason I came today. I'll put a new battery in."

"You don't have to," she said, turning away from the stove. "I called the garage and—"

"It's no bother. I picked up a new one at Benny's this morning and I'll put it in the Buick for you. The battery will no doubt last longer than the car will."

"You didn't have to do that."

"I know. I decided you need taking care of."

Olivia glared at him. "Excuse me, but—"

He held up his hand. "I know you're an independent woman who can do anything you set your mind to. I understand that." He sounded as if he didn't really believe what he was saying. "But you need a little help every once in a while. Every one does."

"I don't need taking care of," she lied. She'd like nothing better than for someone to say *Don't worry, honey, I'll take care of it.* She was tired of taking care of everything by herself, but it was dangerous to depend on Mr. Playboy, even for something as simple as a battery hookup.

"Then you're the only person in the world who doesn't."

"Quit trying to con me. Is that why you sent dinner? Because I needed taking care of?"

"It's in the same category, yes."

Olivia opened her mouth to protest, but no words came out. If he'd been anyone else—that nice, bulky-looking basketball coach or even the mild-mannered accountant—she might have believed him or even welcomed the kindness. But this was Alexander, and she wasn't so sure it would be wise to let him get too close. The man was a skilled charmer, a professional flirt, a natural salesman whose job was to make people think they needed what he had to sell.

"You're looking at me as if I'd just stolen your credit cards."

He was right. She was looking for excuses to back away from a perfectly decent offer of help. What was she—some kind of jerk? He was offering to solve a problem—a big problem—for her, and all she could think about was her silly suspicions.

"I'm being rude. Of course, I appreciate the help with the car. How much was the battery?"

Alex looked for a moment as if he wasn't going to tell her, then changed his mind. "The receipt's in the trunk. I'll give it to you later."

"Thank you, Alex."

He surprised her again by kissing her lightly on the mouth. "You're welcome."

Still, Olivia thought, turning back to the stove, it was wise to stay on her toes where Alex was concerned. Alex—charming, sexy Alex—was a confirmed bachelor, not the kind of man who would be attracted to a woman who came with strings attached. Especially a woman with as many strings as she possessed. Once the novelty wore off, he'd be riding off into the sunset. She'd seen that movie before.

ALL RIGHT, Alex muttered, pacing in the cold in front of Olivia's beat-up Buick. So he'd planned to go on with his life as if he'd never met Olivia Bennett. That was last week. Two weeks ago he'd devised another plan: to circumvent the existence of the children by pretending they didn't exist. He'd figured he could have the woman and ignore the kids.

That plan had fizzled yesterday when he'd found himself painting earrings. Plus, it was difficult for a man to ignore a puddle of soda on his crotch.

Even harder to ignore was his attraction to Olivia. She was quite a woman—she managed to handle her job, family and business with the utmost patience. He didn't know about her work for Judd, though he'd heard Judd praise her even temperament and dependability. Judd didn't give out praise easily.

So it was time for Plan C. If he wanted to be with Olivia he'd have to be with her—in her house, on her terms. Well, maybe not exactly on her terms. She hadn't even agreed to see him.

So here he was on a Saturday afternoon, waiting in the driveway for Wolf to find a wrench. If the giant didn't know how to change a battery, he was about to learn. If he already knew, then he could provide some assistance. Alex thought of his own father and was glad his high school had offered an auto shop class. Dad hadn't been around enough to teach him anything but how to order from a menu and that there was no such thing as happily ever after.

Wolf returned with the proper tools and handed them to Alex. "Nice car," he said, jerking his head toward the Ferrari.

"Thanks. Pop the hood on this, will you?"

Wolf opened the door of the Buick and released the latch. Alex lifted the heavy hood and looked inside. "You know much about cars?"

Wolf looked sheepish. "Not a whole lot."

That was male talk for "nothing." Alex tapped the battery with the wrench. "Let's get this baby out of here. Take this and start with the nuts on the battery cables—counterclockwise."

Olivia stood at the living-room window and watched the two men bend over the engine. It was a strange sight, seeing Wolf working with another man. Olivia had hated being an only child and still did, especially since after Jack's death there'd been no uncles or cousins to take over as male role models. Jack's divorced sister in New Jersey sent the kids birthday cards and Christmas presents, which Olivia appreciated. The children should have some sense of family. Her own father had died two years ago and her mother, heartbroken but self-sufficient, had stayed in Miami in her friendly retirement community. She headed north for occasional visits, but preferred keeping in touch by telephone because she hated to fly.

Olivia missed her. The children's winter break was coming up soon, and the Buick would never make it to Florida, even if Olivia could have afforded the vacation. And Judd would have a heart attack if she left in the middle of tax season. But the urge to run was strong, and as Olivia stood at the window, looking at the handsome man handing her son a wrench, she knew exactly what she was so afraid of: that Alexander Leeds would charm himself right inside her lonely little heart.

6

"WHAT ARE YOU DOING tomorrow?" Alex stood at the kitchen sink and rinsed his hands under the running water.

Olivia handed him a paper towel. "Not much. I usually catch up on laundry and shop for groceries. Sunday's sort of a family day around here. Why?"

Perfect. She'd fallen right into his hands. "Why don't we all go to the movies?" Alex smiled, pleased to have achieved a casual, sincere tone.

Olivia frowned; those big blue eyes gazed at him as if she couldn't believe what she'd heard. "All?"

"Unless you'd rather the two of us went out alone." That sounded even better, Alex decided. Maybe Plan C wouldn't have to be used. Back to B, not a moment too soon.

"No," she said quickly. Too quickly. "But why?"

Alex shrugged. "I thought it would be fun. We'll be working together a lot. We may as well get to know each other better." How hard could it be to act like an uncle for a few hours? Maybe paternal instincts were grossly overrated, after all.

"*All* of us," she repeated, eyeing him with suspicion.

"*All* of us," he assured her. It was time to lay on the guilt. "Unless you don't think any of the children would enjoy going to the movies . . ."

"It's not that. They'd love it, except—"

"Except what?"

"Mmm, nothing."

"Fine. Tell you what, I'll come by around noon and we'll look over the Sunday paper and decide which movie to see."

"Let me make sure I have this right. You want to take the entire Bennett family to the movies tomorrow afternoon to . . . get to know us better?"

He shrugged. "Call it professional relations."

"I don't think I want to call it anything but crazy."

"That's not very nice, Olivia."

She looked guilty for a second, then smiled at him. "You're right. I'm sorry."

"So? We're on for tomorrow?"

"I think so. Sure."

"Great." Alex left quickly. He'd gotten what he wanted. Now all he needed was some professional advice. First he stopped at D'Angelos for an Italian sub to take home for dinner. Once home, he opened a cold can of beer, took his sandwich to the den and turned on the television to see what basketball game was being shown. Then he kicked off his shoes and dialed Judd's house, using Judd's private line.

The phone rang once before Judd's preoccupied greeting. "Hello."

"Judd, it's Alex."

"Hey! If you're calling about income taxes, yours aren't done yet."

"I didn't call about that."

"You're scheduled for March, aren't you?"

"I didn't call about that," Alex repeated. "Relax."

"Everyone in South Kingstown has called me. What, then?"

"I need some personal advice." There was a silence on the other end of the line. "Judd?"

"The last time you needed my personal advice was in sixth grade, when Amy D'Agostino had the first coed birthday party. That was such a success you've been on your own ever since. And done quite well, too."

"Judd, for Christ's sake, I'm serious."

"All right," he drawled. "I'm listening."

"What's a good movie to take kids to see?" In the ensuing, deepening silence, Alex decided he'd better clarify his question. "A family movie."

"A family movie." Judd cleared his throat. "Why?"

"Where's Polly?"

"She and the kids are in town. Why do you have to be so damn mysterious?"

"Plan C. I can't get anywhere with Olivia, so I've decided to do it her way."

"Hey, Leeds. The lady is a friend of mine." There was more than a hint of warning in Judd's voice. "And the last thing I knew it was strictly business between the two of you. Maybe you should keep it that way."

"Believe me, Judd. I've tried. But there's something about her..." Alex thought of those blue eyes, that soft skin. "She thinks I'm some sort of sex-crazed play-boy."

"You are."

"I used to be, years ago. Before AIDS. Before an unprotected one-night stand meant risking my life. In the past few years I've done more looking than anything else."

"I'll believe it when I see it."

Alex ignored the sarcasm. "A movie, Judd. Any ideas?"

"Uh-uh. We rent them, we don't go to them. Look at the paper."

"I did, but the only thing I wanted to see is the new Schwarzenegger film."

"Not for women, though."

"Right."

"Well," Judd said, "you're the expert when it comes to women, buddy. Just don't screw around with Olivia. Why don't you just sell a lot of earrings, so she can send her son to college, and leave her alone?"

"It's not that easy," Alex replied, feeling his heart sink to his big, bare toes as he considered what he was about to admit. "I'm suffering."

"In that case," his friend drawled, failing to disguise his amusement. "I wish you all the luck in the world. You're going to need it."

THE CHOICES were staggering. Alex spread the entertainment section of the newspaper across the dining room table. Olivia and her children leaned forward to read it.

Alex pointed to the Showcase Cinema advertisement. "Surely there must be something we could all enjoy. Aren't there a dozen movies there?"

Olivia shook her head. She had a bad feeling about this, just the same way she felt when he'd broached the subject yesterday. "Nancy's only ten. It has to be rated PG."

Josh moaned. "Mom, nothing's PG anymore, unless it's some dumb cartoon."

Nancy pointed to the small print. "*Wild Horses of Rio Grande?*"

Silence greeted that suggestion. Olivia knew that Wolf and Josh couldn't stomach Nancy's taste in horse movies and she doubted that Alex could hack it, either. "I don't think so," she said, hoping Nancy wouldn't argue. "The movie should be something we'd all like to see."

Alex turned to the teenager. "What about it, Wolf? Any suggestions?"

"Nope. I'm stayin' out of this one."

Olivia saw that Alex looked as if he wished he could stay out of it, too. "Give up?"

Alex shook his head. "Let's get organized." He took the paper and folded it to the section of alphabetical listings of every movie being shown in the state of Rhode Island. "I'm going to read the titles. Say yes, no or maybe."

"Alex, I don't—"

Wolf interrupted his mother. "Let's try it, Mom. It might work."

Alex looked at Olivia and raised an eyebrow. At her nod, he started reading the movie titles—to mixed reactions. By the time he'd finished with the list, the only thing they'd all agreed on was that there wasn't one movie that everyone could see. Alex looked at Olivia and smiled. "You can't say I didn't try."

Olivia stifled a sigh. Suddenly she realized how much she wished the day could have worked as Alex had planned. "I'm sorry. I appreciate your trying, though."

He folded the paper back to its original shape. "We're not through yet."

Olivia recognized the determined slant to his mouth. "We're not?"

"This just calls for a change in plans, that's all."

Wolf leaned against the wall. "Like what?"

Josh sidled close to Alex and looked up at him. "Maybe we can sneak Nancy in to see *Jungle Killer.*"

Nancy protested. "I don't want to see *Jungle Killer!*"

Olivia agreed with her daughter. There was nothing about those violent movies that appealed to her. She preferred comedies, the sillier the better. "What did you have in mind, Alex?"

"Another activity."

"This ought to be good." Wolf crossed his hands in front of his chest, but there was none of the antagonism toward Alex that Olivia had noticed before.

Olivia turned to Alex. "What kind of activity?"

"Golf."

"Golf?" Olivia didn't think she'd heard right. "It's twenty-one degrees out, Alex. In February."

"Golf," he declared, "would be the perfect thing. And good exercise, too."

Even Josh looked as if he figured his hero had lost his mind. "I don't know, Mr. Leeds . . ."

"Call me Alex." Alex grinned at Olivia, then shrugged. "I guess we'll have to take your car. Unless you and I go in mine, and Wolf drives Josh and Nancy."

"I thought this was a family day."

He grinned. "You can't blame me for trying to get you alone. Come on, we'll take the Buick."

"Think we'll make it?"

"I don't know, but we'll have to risk it, won't we?"

"Sure. I guess we will." There were a lot of things to risk right now. Driving around in the Buick was the least of them.

Twenty minutes later, after heading south on Route 1, they approached the outskirts of Westerly, close to the Connecticut border. Alex turned into a shopping center and drove around to the back. He'd stubbornly refused to give out any information about his new plan, though he had muttered a few things under his breath while the car clanked down the highway.

"It needs time to warm up," she'd told him.

"It needs time to die," he'd countered, gripping the steering wheel with gloved hands.

Olivia had grinned at him. "I guess you'll have to make me rich."

He hadn't returned the smile. "Sweetheart, I promise to do my best."

When he parked in front of the building, Olivia peered at the letters painted on the window. "*Indoor* miniature golf?"

"Sure."

"I've never heard of it."

"It's new. The kids were talking about it at Nancy's party."

"Cool." Wolf apparently approved.

"Can I be on Mom's team?" Nancy scrambled to get the door open.

"Let's go inside first."

The large room was set up as a miniature golf course. Not a bit of floor space was wasted. Beyond a picket fence a couple of pool tables stood in a corner near the snack bar.

Olivia watched Josh position himself next to Alex by the counter. Alex pulled his wallet from the back pocket of his jeans and quickly paid admission, then called to her.

"Want to pick out your club?"

"Sure." She watched him shrug off his leather jacket. She had to give the guy credit. He was handsome as sin, standing there in his teal sweater and soft denim jeans. She'd give anything to know why he'd planned this family outing. What on earth was he hoping to accomplish?

"Let me have your coat," he said, stepping closer. His fingers grazed her shoulders as he helped her slip off the heavy garment. The kids followed him to a row of hooks near the entry, hung up their jackets, and Nancy ran back to take her mother's hand.

"We hafta pick out our clubs. Alex said."

"Fine." She let Nancy tug her toward the males who stood grouped around a stand of golf clubs. "How do we do this—teams?"

Alex grinned and handed her a club. "I think it should be every man for himself."

."Oh, you're the competitive type. I forgot."

"And you're not?"

She tucked her hair behind one ear and smiled at him. "I've never been called competitive, no."

"Well, there's a first time for everything. Maybe you have killer instincts you're not even aware of."

Olivia looked at Alex. There were some things she was all too aware of, like the gleam in his laughing eyes and the appealing slant of his lips as he smiled at her. Her primary response was to block out the rest of the world and have her way with him. He wouldn't put up a fight. She blinked, waiting for common sense to take over. "I don't know much about killer instincts, but I'll bet I can beat you. Miniature golf isn't very difficult."

He raised his eyebrows. "No? I'll give you a three-stroke handicap and five dollars that says you can't win."

"You're on. With no handicap."

"Mom's betting!" Nancy called to her brothers.

Alex stuck out his hand. "Deal."

"Deal." She took it, and its warmth snaked up her arm in seconds. She attempted to tug her hand away but he wouldn't release it. "Alex," she muttered. "Let go."

He looked at her hand enveloped in his and then at her. "I enjoy touching you," he whispered.

He relaxed his grip and Olivia pulled her hand away. "You're just trying to distract me from the competition."

"Sweetheart, competition is the last thing on my mind right now."

Olivia felt her face grow warm. But she flashed him a quick smile and hoisted her golf club. "Don't call me 'sweetheart.' And get ready to lose your money."

They tied at the first shot, a red-roofed doghouse. Alex made it through the windmill in two shots, but Olivia struggled, taking two extra shots. She made up for it on the castle, though. The kids had a blast. Wolf teased Nancy mercilessly, while Josh took forever to set up each shot. Olivia noticed that Alex's concentration was beginning to deteriorate.

"I'm gonna be the big loser," Nancy complained.

Josh handed her ball to her. "So, what else is new?"

Olivia ignored Nancy's protest and aimed her own little yellow ball toward the steep incline of a wooden footbridge. She swung and the ball bounced exactly where she'd planned, over the bridge. From the expression on Alex's face Olivia knew she'd come close to the hole on the other side. She walked around the bridge to look. Six inches away.

"Nice," Alex said. "But you're still two strokes away from beating me."

She putted it in, making it look easy. "We're on the fourteenth hole now. There's time."

"Maybe," he said. "Maybe not."

"You're not nervous, are you?"

He tweaked her hair. "Never."

"That's what I thought. Can I have my handicap back?"

"Not on your life, Bennett."

"That's what I thought." They waited for Nancy to negotiate the bridge, while the boys went on to the next hole. Nancy's face grew red as the ball continued to avoid going into the hole.

"Can I cheat?" she called. "I don't want to be here anymore."

"Sure," Alex said, smothering a laugh. "Take the max on this one." He took the scorecard and a stubby pencil from his shirt pocket and wrote something down.

Olivia looked over his arm at the line of numbers. "How do I know you're not cheating?"

"I don't *need* to cheat," he said, but tucked the scorecard back into his pocket, nonetheless.

Wolf approached them. "Your turn. Who's up?"

"You go," Olivia said to Alex. She'd switched the order of play; every time she went before him, she had the uncomfortable feeling that he studied her rear end when she bent over. She figured he did it on purpose to rattle her. It was working, too.

Alex looked disappointed, but took his ball and placed it on the tee in front of a runway preceding a wooden flower patch. "Watch out, woman," he growled. "I'm going to run you down and take your money."

Olivia was afraid Alex could take anything he wanted.

"YOU OWE ME FIVE BUCKS," he said, long after the golf game had ended. He'd beaten her soundly on the last two holes, with Wolf coming in second, Olivia third, Josh fourth and Nancy in last place.

"I know." She stayed on the front seat of the Buick beside him while the kids went inside and turned on the lights in the house. Wolf wanted to call Becky, Josh wanted to see the basketball scores, and Nancy had to go to the bathroom. Olivia fished a five-dollar bill out of her purse and handed it to him.

"It was worth it," she said. And she meant it, too. They'd had fun. The kids had—typically—argued about the game, then Alex had bought everyone ice-cream sundaes at Friendly's, a popular restaurant down the street. Olivia hadn't had a banana split in years.

"It was?" He turned toward her, looking surprised as he held out the money.

She had a feeling he wasn't planning to come inside. He probably had a date tonight, and it was only four-thirty. "Sure. I almost beat you. You just had a lucky break on that clown's mouth, that's all."

He was closer than she'd thought. He tilted her chin with his thumb and looked at her lips. "I'd forgotten about that mouth," he said. His head dipped lower and he brushed his lips against hers in a slow, erotic motion.

"Luck," she said when he lifted his mouth a fraction of an inch. She tried to keep her tone light, so he wouldn't know how much his simple flirtation affected her. He was so skilled at this, and she was so damn vulnerable. "That's all it was."

"Skill," he murmured, tasting her lips again. "Pure talent."

Olivia smiled, but Alex didn't retreat. "And you're so modest, too."

"You noticed."

"It's hard not to."

"Did you also notice how warm it is in this car all of a sudden?"

"You're sitting too close."

Alex dropped his hands to her shoulders. "Don't go."

"I have to." She kept her voice light. "And don't you have a date?"

He looked blank. "A date? No."

"Then you should," she declared and slid out of the car. Olivia shut the car door and headed for the house. In a minute the doorbell rang, and when she opened it, Alex stood there, holding out her car keys.

"I'm not driving that beast home."

She took the keys. "Thanks."

"And I don't have a date, but you could change that, if you wanted to."

She could feel herself weakening, grasping at straws. "Look, Alex, don't you have twin stewardesses you could call?"

He shook his head. "Not even one."

"How about one of your businesswomen friends— someone you met at Club Med or wherever you were last month?"

"Nope, nobody," he said cheerfully. "I'm going home alone."

Right. Olivia didn't believe him for a minute. "Well, thanks again for the afternoon."

She hated to see him leave, but on the other hand it was a relief. He didn't need to know how much his kisses affected her, or how much she liked him. That would be foolish. The man was dangerous enough already.

Alex turned the key in the ignition and waited a moment for the Ferrari's engine to warm up. He was a fool, he decided. The afternoon had been a disaster from the very beginning. He'd hoped to impress her with his newfound appreciation of family values. Instead, he hadn't even been able to find a movie everyone agreed upon. Then he'd taken them to a less than fancy indoor game warehouse, where he and the Bennett clan had battled their way through eighteen holes. He should have let the boys win. He shouldn't have challenged Olivia.

The ice cream had been a lucky guess, except for the fact that it was fifteen degrees outside. Olivia hadn't stopped shivering the whole time they were at Friendly's. Damn. He'd even taken her five dollars.

Nothing about the day could be called a success.

OLIVIA WAITED until her lunch break on Wednesday to call Alex with the bad news. Despite all their hard work and planning, the bank had turned down the opportunity to loan Glitter Girl enough capital to start production.

"Alex?"

"Hello. What's up?"

"They said no." She couldn't keep the disappointment out of her voice, no matter how unprofessional it sounded.

"They didn't ask for further information?"

"No."

"Well, things are tough for the banks right now. Look," he said. She heard the rustle of papers in the background. "I'll come over tonight around seven. We'll go over our options."

"My only option is to forget the kit and keep making earrings the way I always have. You'll have to send me a bill for the consulting fee."

Alex seemed to ignore her words. "I'll come over tonight," he repeated. "We'll talk then."

"I'd rather come to your office." At least there the children wouldn't hear her disappointment.

"Fine. Do you know where it is?"

"The office complex on Salt Pond Road?"

"That's it. D-6."

"Thanks, Alex." She heard the click in her ear as he hung up the receiver. She needed to copy fourteen tax returns by three, before the mail went out. Beth, her assistant, was off work with a cold. The phone rang continuously, but Judd remained cheerful, whistling whenever he came into the outer office to drop another pile of papers upon her desk.

By the time she finished at five-thirty, all she wanted to do was pick up something easy for dinner, collapse upon her bed and spend the evening feeling sorry for herself. But there wasn't time. She threw together a mess of scrambled eggs and toast for dinner and explained to the kids that she had a meeting with Alex in

Wakefield tonight. Busy with their schoolwork, they didn't ask any questions.

Alex's office was one of many set along a wide, C-shaped driveway. Olivia was familiar with the complex. Her dentist worked here, and for two years Judd's offices had been located here, too, until he'd built something larger in the middle of town.

The glass door was locked, but lights were on inside, so Olivia rang the bell. She heard Alex's quick footsteps, then saw him as he approached the door and fiddled with the lock.

"Hi," he said, his smile warming her. "I've been waiting for you."

"I'm sorry to keep you at the office so late. Maybe we should have done this on the phone." Despite her apologetic words, she was ridiculously glad to see him. Alex's suit jacket was nowhere to be seen, his white shirt was unbuttoned at the collar, and the silk maroon print tie looked as if it had been loosened several times. Olivia had an overwhelming desire to lean into his wide, solid chest and cry her eyes out. Instead she blinked several times and pretended to look around the office.

Alex gestured toward a wide desk. "Paula's, my secretary's. I'm sure you've talked to her by phone." He opened a beige door and gestured down the hallway. "Let's go into my office," he said. "I made a fresh pot of coffee. I thought we might need it."

Olivia followed him. "No coffee, thanks."

"What's the matter?"

"I'm feeling a little . . . beat-up."

He looked surprised, then sympathetic. "Come on," he said, leading her down the hall and into a large room done in muted creams and greens, with blind-covered windows and a walnut desk. She sank into one of the chrome and emerald chairs that faced the desk.

Alex hesitated, then sat down behind the desk and leaned forward. "We—Glitter Girl—have other options." His voice was gentle. "Do you want to take off your coat and hear about them?"

Olivia realized how she must look and the thought made her smile. "All right." She shrugged off her coat and draped it over the back of the chair.

"Coffee?"

It would give her something to do besides wring her hands, she decided. "Please." She watched as he slid his chair to a counter two feet from the desk, poured coffee into two thick mugs and leaned across his desk to place one in front of her. "That should help."

"That's the second bank that's turned down my application, Alex." She cradled the mug in her hand, being careful not to burn herself. "What's wrong with Glitter Girl? Is it the bank's problem or something I can fix?"

"Don't take it personally—it's just business. I've been thinking," he started, then sipped his coffee. "Don't say anything until I've finished."

"Okay."

"I'd like to invest in Glitter Girl myself. I've done the research, and although there's always a risk in any new—"

"Alex! You can't do that."

He frowned. "You're not supposed to say anything until I've finished." She closed her mouth and waited. She'd have a lot to say when he finished, all right. "There's always a risk in any new business, but I know you and know the product. It's a chance for both of us to make some money."

"You really believe in it that much?"

"I do."

Olivia looked at him and wished she could read minds. "We'd be partners?"

"Partners," he repeated. "Has a nice ring to it, don't you think?"

"I'm not sure." Alexander Leeds as a consultant was one thing, but Alexander Leeds as a business partner was not something to be comprehended in two minutes. "I wonder how well we'd work together."

"How has it been so far?"

Olivia thought about his question. To be fair, she would have to say that he'd done what he'd promised. "I guess so far, so good. But what's in it for you?"

He nodded. "An opportunity to make some money— not right away, of course, but down the line. I'm impressed with your company, Olivia. I have been from the start. I'd like to invest in it. It's as simple as that."

As simple as that? What on earth was he thinking of? Olivia studied his expression. He didn't look like a man who took foolish risks, and he said he believed in the product. "I thought you didn't want to mix business and pleasure. You made that awfully clear."

"Business *is* pleasure," he replied softly, the teasing light once again in his eyes. "Especially if it's your business I'm working on."

Olivia didn't quite believe his flattery, but yet . . . There wasn't anything to prove that he didn't mean it. "You've come a long way."

"What do you mean?"

"It's a stretch from a man who didn't want to work with children to a man who now wants to invest in a family-run business."

Alex stood and stepped around the desk. "What I want to do right now," he told her, his dark eyes gleaming, "is take you into my arms and kiss you until you stop reminding me of how wrong I was."

"I love hearing you admit you were wrong, but . . ." Olivia set the mug upon the desk and stood up. "I think I'd better go."

He stopped her, putting one gentle hand upon her shoulder. "There were sparks when we met, Olivia."

"I really don't—"

He hushed her with his mouth. His hands cradled her face, keeping her mouth against his while he took what he wanted from her lips. Olivia felt the familiar heat course through her body as he held her, and forgot all the reasons why she shouldn't be in Alex's arms. It was wonderful to be held, and the man doing the holding exercised a dangerous attraction that she couldn't resist.

She didn't want to.

Olivia reached up to touch his face, and when she did, Alex's tongue swept along the seam of her lips and parted them. It felt like heaven, she thought for one fleeting moment, until she could think no longer.

He felt so good, the heat beneath his shirt touching her, warming her as she slid her hands around his waist to hold him close.

Alex lifted his mouth from hers. "There," he murmured. "Now you won't say 'I told you so.'"

Olivia couldn't say another word. How could he be so controlled and calm when she felt as if she'd been turned inside out? She rested her forehead on his shirt-front and closed her eyes, hoping that when she spoke, her voice would sound normal. But the rapid beat of Alex's heart belied his controlled words. Olivia stood there and held him, tightening her hold around his waist, stroking lightly with the palms of her hands. The heartbeat quickened, making her aware of how much her touch affected the man in her arms.

She decided it was time to back away. However much as she wanted to be held, she still had to back off from this man.

He didn't try to stop her.

Olivia turned and picked up her coat and her purse. She started to say something, but no words came out. She left the room, hoping Alex wouldn't stop her, praying he would.

He didn't. Olivia escaped into the cold and darkness and hurried to her car.

She worried all the way home, first down the empty stretch of Route 1, and then as far as the familiar turn onto Matunuck Beach Road. It had been so long since a man had wanted her, had so obviously desired her. There was a dangerous element in that desire. How easily Alex could tap into the need she felt to be held and loved and wanted!

Since the night she'd met him, she'd sensed something between them. One of those man-woman things, but still . . . there was nothing wrong with the feeling. Just the disappointment over his cool withdrawal when he'd met her family, then his flirting over dinner, then his demands that the children not be included in the business, and his changing of the company's name.

Olivia wished she could go back to that magical evening before Christmas when they'd met.

She was such a fool to run away from him tonight, but didn't know if she'd do things any differently if she could go back and start over again. She should have kissed him for as long as she wanted, until she'd had her fill and gotten the need of him out of her system.

Easier said than done.

7

"Mom, TELL US you're kidding," Wolf begged, tossing the car keys into the air and catching them in the palm of his large hand. He was visibly anxious to drive to Becky's house and work on a history paper.

"I'm not kidding." She sank back into the green rocker and made herself comfortable. "Alex wants to buy into the business. He thinks we're a good investment, even if the banks don't agree."

Josh lay horizontal on the couch. "Do we have to vote on this?"

"I don't know," Olivia answered, "but I need to know how you two feel about it. I didn't want to tell you that the bank turned us down until I talked with Alex. He told me what he wanted to do."

Josh reached for a pencil and paper from a stack of newspapers on the coffee table. "How much money is he willing to invest?"

"Exactly what he asked the banks to loan us." Wolf let out a long whistle, and Olivia nodded. "It's a big decision for us."

"No kidding."

"I'm voting yes," Josh said. "We need the money or we don't have a business."

"That true, Mom?"

"That just about sums it up," she agreed.

"Guess we don't have any choice."

"There's always a choice," she said. "We can try other banks. We can sell stock. We can forget the whole idea and stay with the business of making earrings."

"I vote for Alex." With that, Wolf tossed the keys once more, caught them and then, still whistling, left the room.

"Don't be too late," Olivia called. "Remember it's a school night."

Josh looked at his mother and shrugged. "He's easier to get along with lately, don't you think? Dating Becky has made a new man out of him."

"Once again your wisdom astounds me," she said, climbing out of the chair. She bent and kissed him on the forehead. "Good night, hon. I'm going to bed."

THE NEXT WEEK SPED BY. Olivia and Alex managed the details of the investment process, everyone remained busy making earrings for Valentine's Day, and the progress on the kit seemed to snowball. Each day brought new decisions and new ideas. Alex fielded all problems with great skill and tact, amazing Olivia with his ability to delegate authority and make decisions.

It almost seemed too easy, Olivia noticed the following Friday; she was growing comfortable with the new business relationship. As long as it stayed strictly business, she'd be fine.

Until Valentine's Day. Alex appeared at seven. It was no surprise—he always stopped by after work to discuss the day's progress or problems.

"Happy Valentine's Day," Alex said, holding out a long white box.

"What is this for?" Surprised by the gift, Olivia took the box and held it awkwardly.

"I just told you—Valentine's Day." he closed the door behind him and unbuttoned his coat. "Open it."

Olivia lifted the lid and peeked inside. Pink roses nestled in a cloud of baby's breath. "They're beautiful, Alex." She felt the heat in her face. "I—I'm overwhelmed," she stammered. "Thank you."

"You're welcome." He looked around the living room as he removed his coat and tossed it over the back of the rocker. "It's pretty quiet. Where is everyone?"

"Tonight's the Sweetheart Dance at the high school and also Josh's junior high dance. Nancy's spending the night with Judd's daughter again." Olivia headed towards the kitchen and he followed her. She pulled a vase from underneath the sink and filled it with water.

"That leaves you and me," he said.

Olivia looked at him and smiled. "Since it's Valentine's Day, shouldn't you have a date?"

"Yes. You owe me dinner," Alex said.

"What?" Olivia didn't have a decent portion of food in the house. Tomorrow was Saturday; she'd planned to shop for groceries in the morning. She arranged the roses in the vase and leaned forward to inhale the scent.

"Because I delivered earrings all week without complaining, and gold glitter ruined one of my best white shirts."

"I'll give you dinner tomorrow night," she said, "after I buy some food."

Alex shook his head and moved closer. "No—I don't want to wait."

Olivia backed away. If he started kissing her again, she didn't know how she'd make herself stop. "I'm in the middle of cleaning up downstairs." She headed for the stairs. "You can argue with me while I work, all right?"

Without waiting for an answer, she went downstairs with Alex close behind. There she showed him the new green earrings she'd designed for Saint Patrick's Day— nickel-sized clovers dusted in green glitter and white rhinestones.

"Clever," he said, holding the egg carton to the light. "Limited market, of course."

"The smaller gift shops love seasonal gifts like that," she said, defending her creations.

Alex set the carton back on the card table and shoved his hands into his pockets. "I'm sure they do, Olivia, but we were talking about dinner. Valentine's Day. Romance. Do you remember?"

"I remember there's no food upstairs."

"I don't care about food. I want to be alone with you."

She flashed him a quick smile. "You'll have to get out your little black book and celebrate the holiday with someone else."

"No." He stood up and leaned over her while she swept glitter into the dustpan. "Only with you."

When she turned around to protest, he silenced her with a kiss. The glitter spilled back onto the floor as Olivia relaxed her hold on the dustpan.

"You shouldn't—" she said against his mouth, but he kissed her again; this time he grabbed her shoulders and held her upright so she couldn't back away.

The kiss ended after a long moment, leaving the two of them shaken. Olivia didn't step away this time. She even forgot about the dustpan and it clattered to the floor.

"Now," he murmured, still holding her. "What were you saying about Valentine's Day?"

"I don't remember."

"Good," he said, and claimed her mouth once again.

Olivia enjoyed touching him. Her hands roamed his back, savoring the warmth she found there.

"Come home with me," he urged. "There's lots of food at my house."

"But . . ."

"No excuses." Alex lifted her chin. "The kids are out, and it's just the two of us."

"I have to pick up Josh at ten."

Alex looked at his watch. "It's only seven-thirty. That's enough time for me to cook for us."

"You're going to cook?"

"I can try. Since you're not cooperating, I'm going to the next available solution."

"Maybe we'd better go out."

"No—I want you all to myself. Besides, you've never seen my house."

"I drove by it once," she confessed. "It wasn't what I'd pictured."

"Which was?"

"A modern condominium with a view of the ocean."

He grinned. "I'll admit that was tempting, until I saw the For Sale sign in front of a large Victorian in town." He pulled her closer. "Come home with me. I'll cook for you and give you a tour."

"I sense an ulterior motive behind the invitation," she teased.

"I just want to be alone with you."

That was what Olivia wanted, too. Although being alone with Alex probably wasn't the most intelligent thing she would ever do, it would definitely go down as the most fun.

They hopped into the Ferrari and stopped at the supermarket for the dinner ingredients. Alex did as he'd promised, leading Olivia through all three stories of the old house, surprising her with a home filled with an appealing combination of country charm and modern conveniences. They ate at the small, round oak table in the kitchen.

"Now will you admit this was a good idea?" Alex asked, clearing the plates from the table and dumping them into the sink.

"Absolutely." Olivia refilled her wineglass. "Roses and dinner. A perfect holiday."

Alex returned to the table, and Olivia felt his fingers slide through her hair, sending tiny tremors along her spine. His lips grazed the back of her neck, and she shivered. "You have a gorgeous neck," he whispered.

"You're trying to seduce me again."

He let her hair drop and sat down near her. "Nothing so simple, I assure you. Seduction is the least of my intentions," he said, a smile on his handsome face.

"Really?"

"Uh-huh. I want more than just one night. I want lots of nights with you. With you," he said emphatically, his dark eyes holding her gaze, "in my bed."

Olivia swallowed. It had been such a long time since she'd made love with a man. After Jack left, she hadn't had the heart to risk being hurt again. It sounded trite, but it was the truth just the same. Frightened was the way she felt whenever Alex came too close, when he helped Wolf and Josh or laughed at Nancy's antics.

Terrified was how she felt when he touched her. And yet she loved his touch.

Olivia tried to smile. "I'm sorry, Alex. But that's not in the marketing plan." *Neither is falling in love with my new business partner.*

"What happened to your husband? Judd said you're a widow, but he wouldn't tell me anything else."

Olivia took a sip of her wine. "My husband left me for another woman, but had a heart attack before the divorce. That was a few years ago, and it doesn't hurt anymore."

"I'm sorry, Olivia."

"Thank you, but it happened a long time ago—at least, it feels as if it was a long time ago."

Alex smiled and took her hand. "Well, if you're not going to get into my bed, then come into the den and sit on the couch with me for a while. We can watch a movie."

Olivia glanced at her watch. "I don't have time. I have to be at the junior high at ten, and it's almost nine now."

He stood up and lifted her to her feet. "We'll watch something, and you can take the tape home and finish seeing it." He led her down a wide hallway, through the living room with its high ceilings and tall windows, to a corner room. "Here." He gestured toward a cabinet near the oversize television. "Pick a movie."

She went over and opened the door, amazed by the quantity of tapes. It was a movie addict's dream, but couldn't be compared to the temptation of climbing into bed upstairs with Alex.

"I WANT YOU TO COME."

"That's impossible, Alex."

"Nothing is impossible," he insisted, counting heart-shaped findings into a plastic pouch. "You're simply being stubborn."

Olivia shrugged and turned back to sorting purple rhinestones from white ones. She planned to work all morning, and then, since it was Saturday, take Josh and Nancy to the Wakefield Mall to look for sales at the shoe store. "I was born stubborn."

He muttered something under his breath, but Olivia couldn't catch the words. Finished with the bag, he sealed it with a staple and reached for another. "It's good business."

"Then you go."

"Come with me. It's the toy fair, for God's sake. It's your business. You'll learn a lot."

"Alex, I can't go off to New York and leave everything here."

"'Everything' means the children."

"Them and the business."

"It's just a long weekend, Olivia. Surely you've gone away for weekends before?"

Not alone with a gorgeous man who makes my knees tremble when he walks into the room. Olivia decided not to respond. She wanted to say yes to the trip, but didn't think it would be the smartest thing she'd ever agreed to.

But Alex clearly wasn't the type to give up easily. "You have, haven't you?"

"No," she admitted, putting down the bag of rhinestones. She couldn't pretend she was working any longer. She looked him right in the eye and glared. "I haven't had the time, money or inclination to leave my family."

"Meaning there hasn't been a man in your life you've wanted to be alone with?"

"That is none of your business. And it's none of your business whether or not I leave my kids."

"You don't have to sound as if they'd wither away and die if you weren't here," Alex countered. "You should have some fun. And you could use a vacation."

"I really can't—" she began, but he cut her off.

"All right. Forget thinking of it as a vacation. How about the fact that you'd be meeting people in the business? Making contacts? You'd enjoy the toy fair, you know. And we could even see a Broadway show."

"It's not in the company's budget."

"That's no excuse, sweetheart. I always go, so my own company is paying the tab. I've booked a suite at the Marriott downtown, so you're free to share it, if that makes you feel better."

Olivia didn't see how sharing a suite with Alex could make her feel better. It would be torture. He'd flirt, she'd flirt back, the bed would be only a few feet away and...

"Besides," he continued. "There are people I'd like you to meet."

"I can't, Alex."

"Can't—or won't?"

"I *can't* leave three kids for the weekend."

He frowned, the fury in his eyes turning them a shade of chestnut. "You're hiding behind the kids again, Olivia."

"That's not fair, Alex."

"It's quite fair. It's what you do whenever I get too close to you. Maybe it's what you do when anyone gets too close, I don't know— I'm just speaking from personal experience. You use those kids like some kind of damn wall."

Olivia opened her mouth to protest, but couldn't deny the truth.

THE AMTRAK TRAIN rattled and swayed west, stopping occasionally in Connecticut to pick up passengers. A heavy pillow of tension filled Olivia's insides, tying her stomach in knots. She watched the scenery alongside the railroad tracks and figured this could be the stupidest thing she'd ever done in her life.

Maybe she should have stayed home.

She knew from talking to Alex's secretary that he'd left Thursday. And here she was, Friday afternoon, heading to New York.

She didn't know what would happen when she arrived at the Marriott in New York, but had made up her mind that she would see the toy fair and not worry about anything else.

IT WAS AFTER SEVEN when Alex heard the small knock on the door. "Yes?" he called.

"It's Olivia," was the muffled reply.

"Olivia?" Alex hurried to open the door but couldn't think of a single thing to say. He simply stared at her. She looked gorgeous in her slim black dress and black stockings. She held her coat over her arm and beside her on the floor was a small suitcase.

"I decided to come to the toy fair," she said, as if it were the most natural thing in the world. He stepped back and let her enter, then grabbed her suitcase and moved it inside before shutting the door. Relief made him dizzy, a whiff of her perfume threatened to knock him to his knees.

"You *what?*" he managed.

"You offered me a place to stay, remember?" Her voice was soft, and the unguarded expression in her blue eyes entranced him.

"Yes," he croaked. "Of course."

"You do have an extra bedroom, don't you?"

"Yes," he said and took a deep breath, suddenly feeling as if the world had settled and put him in exactly the right place at the right time. He wasn't going to argue with fate—or even give it a chance to complicate a weekend that had just developed endless and exhilarating possibilities. Alex came close to Olivia and put his hands upon her shoulders. "But you don't have to use it."

"Alex—" she began, but he smothered her with kisses until she started to laugh. He held her and felt the tension ease out of her. She rested her head against his chest while he stroked her hair.

"What made you change your mind?"

"You did." She sighed. "You were right, you know. I do hide behind the children."

"I'm glad you do. Until now, that is."

"Why?"

"Less competition for me to drive off."

"I guess that's one way to look at it."

"Look at me," he said. She raised her head. "Tell me why you came here, came to me."

"To be with you." A simple answer, yet one filled with so many conflicting emotions.

"Why are you shaking?"

Olivia had promised herself the freedom to be honest. "Because I'm scared to death, that's why."

"Scared of me?"

"No," she admitted. "Not you."

"Then what?"

"Something inside of me—a part that says 'Don't do it, Olivia. Stay by yourself, where you're nice and safe.'"

"You're safe with me," he promised, and there was no laughter in his eyes, no teasing smile.

"Yes," she answered, reaching to touch his face. She ran her finger along his jaw, then touched his bottom lip. "I'd like to believe that."

"Now might be a good time to start."

She stood on tiptoe to kiss him lightly on the lips, enjoying the unaccustomed feeling of freedom. "You have a dinner planned with Hasbro."

He frowned. "How did you know that?"

"Paula told me. I needed to know if I could get into this suite or not."

"I'll cancel," he said.

"No. It's important."

"Come with me."

"All right."

"It will be a quick dinner."

"No dessert?"

"We'll have it here later."

"Much later."

"I don't want to wait."

Olivia looked at her watch. "We only have ten minutes."

"That means," he said, pulling her into his arms and holding her tightly against his body, "I can kiss you for eight minutes and then tie my tie."

"Sounds like a good plan to me," she murmured, pulling his head down to hers.

IN A LARGE PARTY of thirteen, it wasn't difficult for Alex and Olivia to leave before the second round of coffee.

"We have an early breakfast meeting," Alex said, and the rest of the people around the table nodded. Everyone knew how much business needed to be conducted in a short amount of time.

"That was easy," Olivia said later, snug in the taxi as it sped through the dark city streets.

Alex took her hand. "I told you so."

Suddenly nervous, Olivia looked out the taxi window. "Isn't it incredible how many people are still walking around the streets?"

"The Broadway shows are just getting out," he explained. Olivia saw the brightly lit marquees advertising shows she'd only heard about on television. New York looked exciting and fast and foreign. "I'd ask you if you wanted to walk around, but I don't know how safe it is."

The taxi pulled up in front of the Marriott, Alex helped Olivia out of the cab and paid the driver. They held hands and walked through the bright lobby as if they were an old married couple. The wait for the elevator seemed interminable, but eventually they stepped out on the tenth floor and Alex opened the door of the suite.

One corner lamp cast a cozy glow over the room. Champagne waited in an ice bucket on the coffee table between a pair of mint-green love seats. A platter held an array of cheeses, fruits and crackers, a tall white thermos and two coffee cups nestled on a silver tray beside it.

"What's all this?"

"Dessert," he told her. "I promised you, didn't I?"

"But how did you do this?"

"I placed an order with room service—and guessed at the time." He glanced at the table. "I ordered decaf. Would you like coffee or champagne?"

Olivia doubted that coffee would settle the swarm of jitters that had landed in her midsection while on the taxi, but said, "Coffee, I think." She sat down on the couch and, since Alex was in the process of taking off his suit jacket and loosening his tie, she added, "I'll pour."

"I want to spoil you," he said. "You shouldn't have to lift a finger. This is a vacation for you."

"I thought it was business," she teased, filling the cups with steaming coffee.

"In the daytime," he growled, joining her on the couch. "At night we're off duty."

Olivia smiled. "You've never been a parent," she said. "There is no such thing as 'off duty.'"

"Then I need to take you away more often. You should see how the other half lives."

She sipped her coffee, hoping her trembling hands wouldn't cause her to spill the hot liquid over her lap.

He sat down beside her and reached for his coffee. "There should be dessert underneath that cover." He lifted a silver dome to reveal a plate piled high with sugar cookies. "Just for you."

"You remembered."

"There are lots of things I remember," he whispered, replaced the dome on the cookies and set his cup back on the table without drinking anything. He reached for a lock of her hair that lay swirled on her shoulder. "I remember how your hair shone gold when I first met you."

"You wore a tie with holly leaves all over it."

"Your yellow sweater—the one you wore at our first board meeting—has haunted my dreams."

"I didn't know you were such a romantic person."

He took the cup out of her hands and set it upon the table, too. "Put your arms around me," he ordered, "and I'll prove it."

Olivia turned obediently, tucking one leg beneath her. She slipped her hands behind his head to touch the soft hair at the back of Alex's neck. She smiled into his brown eyes and felt her nervousness soften into a different kind of tension, the kind that made her fingers slip back and forth against his skin. "Well?" she asked, waiting for him to touch her again.

He held her waist and gently tugged her toward him so that she was kneeling beside him. "I thought you admired my business sense."

"I do." She kissed him lightly on the lips. "You're very smart about some things."

"Only some?"

"Well," she conceded, trailing her lips along his cheek. "You do have a good memory."

"You wore this black dress on the night we met."

She didn't bother to hide her surprise. "Yes, I did."

"See?" He fiddled with the zipper at the back of her neck. "I wanted to take you home with me and make love to you until dawn."

"You didn't know I was a mother then, did you? It wouldn't have worked—you didn't date women with children." He looked guilty and she felt sorry for him. "Polly told me."

"Judd has a big mouth."

"I'm glad. It explained a lot about you," she said, stopping when he opened the back of her dress and slid the neckline past her shoulders. Shivers ran through her body. "Alex—"

He planted a kiss upon a waiting shoulder, then looked at her again. "What?"

Olivia kept her hands around his neck, but wished she could avoid his questioning gaze. "Be kind."

He looked perplexed, then understanding lighted his eyes. "You are a gorgeous, sexy, desirable woman. *Kindness* doesn't enter into making love to you. In fact," he said, slipping the bodice of the dress lower to reveal a lace-edged black brassiere, "you'll have to be kind to me, because I'm about to fall apart from wanting you."

"Is that true?" The new lingerie had been worth the price.

He closed his eyes briefly. "Yes, Olivia. That's true."

She slid her hands to his tie. "Then I guess I'd better help you," she murmured, loosening the silk fabric until she'd untied the knot. Then she unbuttoned the first two buttons of his shirt.

Alex stopped her. "You haven't seen the bedroom."

She smiled. "Are you suggesting we move?"

"It's either move or make love to you on a three-foot sofa."

"Move," she said, scooting away from him to stand up. She held up her dress over her breasts and suddenly felt shy.

"Don't," he said, seeming to read her mind. "You're so beautiful." He took her face between his hands and kissed her, his lips warm and demanding. She opened her mouth and let his seeking tongue play with hers, her hands going around his waist to hold him tight; she didn't care that her dress crumpled between them.

"Come on," he said, lifting his mouth from hers.

They made their way across the living room and through an opened door, Alex stopping to kiss her at least three times before Olivia lost count. Somewhere along the way her dress must have slipped to the emerald carpet, with Alex's tie for company.

The bedroom was dark except for a triangle of light that entered from the living room, outlining the large bed. The maid had turned down the covers and placed tiny squares of chocolate upon the pillows, but Olivia, still in the heated circle of Alex's arms, barely noticed. She finally succeeded in undoing the buttons on his shirt; her hands found their way inside to sweep over the furry warmth of his chest while he shrugged his arms from the sleeves and threw the shirt onto the carpet.

"My turn," he whispered, reaching out. His fingers made quick work of the fastener that held her bra together, then he slipped the scrap of black lace down her arms and tossed it away. "God, you're lovely."

Olivia surprised herself; she'd thought she'd be embarrassed, but wasn't. Not anymore. She doubted that a man, even one with Alex's experience, could fake such a look of passion.

"So are you," she said, planting small kisses near his breastbone. The mat of hair on his chest tickled the tips of her breasts.

"There's more," he teased, his voice soft, his hands coming around her waist to hook underneath her panty hose. "As much as I enjoy your legs in black stockings . . ."

His hands lingered on her bare buttocks, cupping the curves in his warm palms before tugging the rest of the fabric over her thighs. Alex knelt before her, and she obligingly lifted one foot at a time so he could peel the hose off her feet. He kissed his way slowly upward, his warm breath caressing her skin. Higher and higher, to the tops of her thighs, until Olivia trembled from wanting more of him than the brief whisper of breath upon her skin.

His lips found her abdomen, then he stopped and stood before her. She reached for his belt buckle, but he swept her hands aside and quickly removed his clothes, faster than her fumbling efforts would have allowed. Then it was skin against skin, his hard warmth against her waiting heat. Her fingers ran along his spine, his caressed her bottom and held her against him.

"The bed," he said, guiding her until she felt the mattress against the backs of her legs. She sat down and moved to one side so that Alex could get in. "Wait," he said, reaching toward the nightstand. A moment later he tossed aside the covers and followed her across the mattress. She knelt near the pillow and reached for him.

Nothing else mattered. His mouth found hers in the semidarkness, and she gripped his shoulders while his tongue delved and played with hers. He seemed to radiate heat, though the rest of their bodies wasn't touching. But within moments she slipped sideways and he joined her, still kissing her mouth. She slid against him, lying on her side, and felt the hard length of him brush her thigh. Over and over again she melted, her body languorous, her skin on fire. It had been a long time since she'd made love with anyone, yet the feeling was achingly familiar. Passion, strong and silent, rose between them.

He urged her closer, and she wrapped a leg over one of his thighs. His fingers danced between her legs, unfolding and exploring. She gripped his shoulders, his hands clutched her bottom, and he entered her, sure and hard and slow.

He filled her, and Olivia gasped against his mouth, yet her body opened willingly, easily, welcoming the intrusion. He moved slowly, in a rhythm meant to fill her more with every move. He tumbled her onto her back, still claiming her mouth, still filling her body until the rhythm took over.

Olivia closed her eyes, caught in a whirl of sensation that rose and built with every movement of Alex's body. He seemed to sense what she needed and gave it to her until she tightened around him. She climaxed, moaning into Alex's mouth, his body bringing her such pleasure that she felt about to break into tiny pieces.

He increased the pressure and lengthened his thrusts until he groaned into her mouth. Delicious aftershocks rippled through her as he came inside her, then stilled, his chest heaving.

They clung together for long moments, until Alex lifted his head and broke the kiss. His lips skimmed her neck to nuzzle her ear. "Sweetheart, we have to do this more often."

Olivia smiled, running her hands along his back. "I think you're right."

He lifted his head to look into her eyes. "You're smiling."

"You sound surprised."

"Surprise is the least of how I feel right now."

"Tell me," she whispered, her fingers touching his bottom lip. He kissed the fingertips that brushed his mouth.

"Amazed. Overwhelmed." He grinned at her, a lock of hair tumbling across his forehead. "Grateful."

"Me, too."

He smiled into her eyes, then rolled her onto her side where, still joined, they kissed again. No more words were necessary for some time, until he eased himself away and pulled the sheet over her bare body. "Stay right there."

"I'm not sleepy," she protested.

"Neither am I, sweetheart. I'm going to get the champagne."

Olivia snuggled into the bed until Alex returned to the room with a bucket filled with ice and a bottle of champagne. He was still naked and seemingly oblivious to it as he popped the cork and poured the champagne into fluted glasses.

Olivia surprised herself again by not feeling self-conscious. She luxuriated in the feel of the sheets against her bare skin. There was such freedom in it all—in the weekend away, in the anonymity of the city hotel, in the pleasure of being a woman in the privacy and delight of sharing a bed with a special man.

Not just any man. Alexander.

Olivia accepted the glass Alex held out and lifted it in a silent toast. Suddenly she felt like celebrating.

8

"To New York," she said.

Alex touched her glass with his own. "To us. And to Glitter Girl's success." He slipped between the sheets and smiled at her. "I dreamed of this," he said. "I've thought about it forever, since the evening I met you, which does seem like a very long time ago."

The champagne tasted wonderful, bubbly and dry. "You always know the right thing to say."

"No, not when it comes to you, I don't."

The right words again. Olivia sipped the champagne. So what if his past contained adventures like sex-filled weekends in New York all the time? It didn't matter. Not tonight, anyway. This was her weekend, with her man—however temporarily. She was determined to enjoy these unusual days.

Alex took her empty glass and put it upon the nightstand, then turned back to her. "Now I'm going to make love to you again, only this time I can love you in ways I've only dreamed of," he declared, his mouth descending. He kissed her, and when he lifted his head to smile down, Olivia's lips felt bruised, a not unpleasant reminder of their previous lovemaking.

"Can I turn the light on?" He had left the door open wider when he returned with the champagne, and the light from the living room cast a glow over the bed.

Though not as shy as she'd felt earlier, Olivia still preferred the shadowy intimacy of the unlit room. "No. I like it this way."

"In the morning, then," he murmured. "I'll see you."

"You'll just have to be content to touch me."

"Oh, that's not a hardship," Alex said. "Not at all." He eased her onto the mattress and spread her hair across the pillow in yellow waves. He explored her skin with his lips and tongue and hands, pulling the sheet back to gain access to the length of her tiny body.

Olivia was on fire with wanting him again. Just the touch of his hands along her skin sent shivers of need and longing through her, centering in the most private places of her body. His tongue found the aching between her thighs, his fingers touched, excited and finally filled her.

"I want to know you," he murmured. "Every inch, every part of you. I need to know what you like and what you don't like."

Olivia moaned, her need rising, and Alex moved his fingers slightly, widening the space between them until she gasped with pleasure. "Yes," she managed to whisper.

His mouth followed the path his fingers had made. "And this?"

"Yes." The exquisite torture of his lips now made her gasp with surprise. It had been a long time, but had it ever been like this? Olivia tried to remember, but her thoughts swirled away, transformed into sensation as Alex's sweet explorations continued. Finally, after long moments, he slid above her and fitted his body into hers.

They took their time, making it last, stopping to kiss and murmur quiet words into each other's ears, moving hard and deep or softly and slowly until, spinning out of control, they rocked together in mindless explosions.

Wrapped in each other's arms, they slept. The sounds of the city at night—sirens, honking horns and loud voices—might as well have been absent. Olivia tucked her cheek against the strong muscle of Alex's arm and never heard a thing.

OLIVIA WOKE AND STRETCHED sleepily, her foot encountering a warm, hairy leg. For a split second she had no idea where she was or why a male body part should be resting near her. She opened her eyes and saw the unfamiliar hotel bedroom, the memory of the previous evening came back and she relaxed.

Alex. New York. Her weekend of sin in the Big Apple had begun. She turned slightly and looked at the man who slept beside her. He lay on his back with one arm thrown over his head, a blanket came to his waist, and the white sheet covered part of his chest. His dark hair was a mess, and the stubble on his cheeks was so uncharacteristic of the impeccable Alexander Leeds that Olivia couldn't resist slipping one arm from the warmth of the covers to run her index finger along his rough chin and feel for herself.

He never moved.

Olivia snuggled back under the covers and listened to the unfamiliar city sounds outside the wide window. She had no idea what time it was, which was a strange feeling, but since she had no idea what the schedule held today, she didn't know whether they were missing anything important. She'd have to let Alex worry about that. Surely he had a plan for the weekend.

Olivia looked forward to the day, no matter what was going to take place. She was away from Rhode Island, freed from responsibilities and able to enjoy the day however she pleased. Whether it was business or pleasure simply didn't matter.

She wondered where her good judgment had gone. Even if this weekend turned out to be a simple fling and nothing more, she would at least have had time to feel loved and desired. Olivia told herself she was foolish to risk her heart, foolish to have fallen in love. She rolled onto her side and admired the man sleeping close to her. Even if she *was* a fool, she'd have one hell of a weekend to remember.

ALEX ROLLED OVER and encountered the hard mattress beneath him. He'd learned long ago to accustom himself to various beds, but he preferred a water bed to any other kind. He tried not to wake up, tried to hang on to the last threads of sleep, but the nagging suspicion that he had something important to do wouldn't let him slip back into unconsciousness. Eyes still closed, he stretched across the wide bed and encountered warmth but no body. He reached farther, hoping to make contact with warm, willing female skin, but the space was empty. Disappointed, Alex opened his eyes. Olivia wasn't there.

Damn. He'd dreamed of waking up with her beside him. Hell, he'd dreamed of waking her up—in the most erotic ways—but his morning fantasies were not coming true. He heard the water running in the shower and flirted with the idea of joining her, but didn't know how she'd feel about sharing it with him. Alex debated the pros and cons and opted for the side of safety; he decided to give the woman some privacy.

The sex had been great. He wanted her again—his body was ready now—but he'd have to go slowly. Last night had been a dream come true. She'd stood at the door of his suite, holding a suitcase, wearing that black dress. She'd made love to him with such giving and open enjoyment. She'd smelled like May flowers, and the scent still clung to the pillowcase next to his.

Alex heard the water stop running and wondered if she'd step into the bedroom wrapped in a towel or if that lush little body would be naked. The thought continued to tantalize him as he heard her move around behind the closed bathroom door.

He closed his eyes, feigning sleep, when he heard the door swing open, but opened them slightly so that he could watch her. She had tucked the white hotel towel around her, revealing only the tops of her breasts and her legs. He still lay, hoping she'd return to bed so he could touch her, kiss her, come inside her.

"Good morning, Alex," she said, laughter in her voice.

He tried to fake waking up. "Mmm?"

She bent over him and kissed his cheek. "I can tell you're faking."

He opened his eyes. "How?"

"I've had a lot of experience at home."

When she began to move away he reached out and grabbed her hand. "Don't go."

"It's after nine. We must have a lot to do."

He shook his head. "Nothing important."

"I don't believe you."

"All right," Alex amended. "I have appointments, but nothing as important as making love with you."

She smiled. "About last night . . ."

"I don't want to talk," he said, tugging her closer. He reached up with his free hand and pulled the towel from her body so that he could touch her breasts. Soft skin and pebbled nipples tempted him to the point where he wouldn't have cared if he was meeting with the president of Toys 'R' Us in five minutes. He wanted Olivia, and from the way she was looking at him, he figured she wanted him, too. He kicked the sheet aside and pulled her closer.

"Alex . . ." she said, but there was no protest in the word, only laughter; she sprawled on top of him.

He kissed one soft breast before looking up. "Yes, Olivia? What do you want?"

She wriggled. "The question is, what do *you* want?"

He stopped smiling; the ache in his groin was almost painful. He lifted her slightly and brought her down on top of him. She took him, sleek and waiting. "This, Olivia," he groaned, holding her hips still until he'd filled her. "Only this."

Later, snuggled together beneath the white sheets, they waited for the breakfast Alex had ordered from room service. "Just bring coffee first," he'd said into the telephone. "And breakfast anytime you get around to it after that."

Olivia wriggled closer. "Have you always been this smart?"

"Not always."

"Were you the kind of boy who always got in trouble or the kind that did everything right?"

"I don't know." He put one arm around her and held her against him.

"What do you mean?"

"I was an only child. My parents were divorced when I was eight. Up until then I had the perfect home—two parents who were always there. I never heard them fight or say an unkind word, except one day my father wasn't living at home anymore. He was always a quiet man, and after the divorce, well, I don't remember much happiness."

Olivia thought she heard warning bells, but decided to risk asking one more question. "Are they still alive?"

"No, they both died several years ago—within three months of each other." He turned away and sat up. "Look, Olivia, there really isn't much to tell. My mother went to work after the divorce, washing dishes in a nursing home down the street. My father wasn't around much. He was in his late forties when I was born, so by the time they divorced he didn't have much connection to me."

"I'm sorry, Alex. But surely they must have loved you very much."

He laughed, but there was no joy in the sound. "Love didn't run in the family, Olivia. Even the happy family routine must have been an act they put on for a small child, until they figured I was old enough to understand divorce. I don't know." He turned to look at her, and there were deep grooves etched in his face that Olivia had never seen before. "My father did his duty and visited me once a month. We'd go out to dinner and make polite conversation. I really think he tried to do his best—but he didn't have it in him.

"I don't believe he didn't love you."

"Believe it or not, it's true. We Leeds men are a cold bunch, I'm afraid." Alex slid out of bed. The laughing, teasing man had gone, replaced by someone cold and bitter. His action surprised her.

"Alex?"

But his attention was claimed by a knock on the door. He slipped into a pair of slacks and left the bedroom. When he returned, he carried a tray with a large carafe of coffee, two cups and a chrysanthemum in a white china vase.

"That was fast," she said, inhaling the smell of the coffee.

He placed the tray carefully on the bed, then sat down on the edge of the mattress while Olivia draped the sheet to cover her nakedness. Alex poured two cups of coffee and handed her one. "The kid who brought the coffee said breakfast wouldn't be too far behind."

"This is enough for now, thanks," she said, taking a cautious sip of the steaming liquid. She wouldn't ask any questions about Alex's childhood now, but Olivia wondered about Alex's memories. She felt he was telling the truth. Was that why typical family life seemed to scare him to death? She thought he'd have craved it after such a barren childhood, instead of claiming he wasn't cut out for happy endings. What was Alex afraid of?

"It was a successful trip," Alex said, snapping his briefcase shut and setting it upon the floor of the train. "We'll send out Glitter Girl samples first thing tomorrow."

"And then?"

"We watch the orders roll in. Meanwhile, I'll keep working on Toys 'R' Us. We may not get them this year, but we're going to keep up the pressure for next year. I'm going to look into mail order, too. Remember?"

"Yes." Olivia leaned back against the hard seat as the train rocked north through Connecticut. It didn't seem possible that it was already Sunday afternoon. The days had gone by in a whirl of hours spent at the toy fair, conversations with retailers, discussions with other manufacturers. But whether they were alone or in the midst of a crowd of business-suited men, the current of awareness had remained strong.

Saturday evening Alex had surprised her with tickets to see *Phantom of the Opera*, and Olivia had cried through most of it, just from the sheer beauty of the music.

They'd drunk champagne and fed each other sugar cookies while watching an old movie on television. They'd made love to each other, learning when to be gentle, learning when not to be. She'd learned other things, too—and had never mentioned the subject of Alex's parents again.

"Tired?"

"Yes."

"Lean against me," he offered, moving closer.

"Yes," Olivia said, snuggling against the shoulder Alex offered. *We're a cold bunch*, he'd said of the Leeds family. Well, this particular Leeds wasn't cold at all. She'd fallen in love with a warm, laughing man who made her feel like a woman again. *I love you, Alex* were words that would remain unspoken, at least for now. But she could show him how much she cared. There were other ways to say *I love you*.

IT HAD BEEN A LONG WEEK. He'd driven home from the train station in Olivia's rattling car and let her take him back to his place. He'd tried to get her to stay for a while—he'd teased her with the idea of his water bed, but naturally she had to get home. *The children,* she'd said, an apology in her voice. *You understand.*

And he'd understood, of course. He just didn't like it. He wanted Olivia all to himself for as many days and nights as it took to satisfy him. But from the way the weekend had gone, it might take a long time.

So Alex patiently trotted through the chores, meetings and paperwork at his office while looking forward to the weekly Friday evenings and Saturday workdays at the Bennett house. He didn't mind the Bennetts, but there was so damn many of them, and he only wanted one.

Friday evening brought him to Olivia's basement, content to unpack cartons of jewelry supplies while plotting how to kidnap Olivia and take her to his house. A moment later he stared at a chocolate-frosted cake topped with flaming candles.

"Happy Birthday!" the children shouted, while Olivia kissed him on the cheek.

Alex realized he'd forgotten his own birthday again. "How did you know?"

Olivia gave him an impish smile. "Nancy told me it was in February, so I looked at your driver's license for the exact date. I didn't expect leap year, though."

"It's easy to forget a birthday when it only comes every four years."

"Aren't you going to blow out the candles?" Nancy urged.

"Don't forget to make a wish," Olivia added.

Alex's answer was to lean toward the cake and blow. Every single candle flickered and went out. "How many were there?"

Nancy grinned. "We used up the whole box."

He groaned. "Thanks a lot—I'm only thirty-four."

Josh picked the candles off the cake and licked the frosting off their bottoms. "Younger than Mom."

Olivia picked up the knife and made the first slice in the cake. "It doesn't bother me—I'm used to being the oldest around here." She plopped a slice of cake onto a small paper plate and handed it to Alex. "You get the first piece."

Alex took it and smiled at her. She handed him a fork and he took a bite of the cake. "Delicious," he pronounced. "I haven't celebrated my birthday in years."

Olivia didn't look surprised. "Well, enjoy."

Cake wasn't exactly what he'd planned to enjoy tonight, but he tried to look pleased as he took another mouthful. Wolf went to the kitchen and returned with a half gallon of ice cream. "You forgot something," he said, setting it upon the table.

Alex put down his plate. "I'll scoop."

"No," Olivia said. "It's your birthday. You're not supposed to do anything."

He looked at her and raised his eyebrows. Her face colored pink, and for a moment he wondered if she was actually talking about serving ice cream. "Really?"

She winked at him, and suddenly Alex began to enjoy himself. Despite the noisy presence of the Bennett children, he had the distinct feeling his birthday wish might yet come true.

"How did you know what I wished for?"

"I'm learning what you like," she whispered, trailing

her lips along his rib cage and lower to his abdomen.

The quiet and isolation of his bedroom contrasted with the raucous house they'd left thirty minutes ago. Alex figured it felt like a hundred years since the weekend, when he'd been able to touch Olivia whenever he pleased. Moments ago she'd wriggled from his grasp and raced him to the bedroom.

He'd let her win.

And now, their clothes scattered all over the carpet, they lay in the middle of his king-size bed while Olivia hummed "Happy Birthday" and enticed him with her lips and tongue.

"It was a long week," Alex groaned.

"Very long," she agreed, touching him with gentle hands until he thought he'd explode.

"Come here," he whispered, reaching for her, letting his fingers tangle in the soft hair that lay draped over his thigh.

She had the audacity to smile. "Not yet."

"*Now.* He'd waited all week to have her again. He couldn't wait any longer. He tumbled her over, wanting her more than he could have believed possible. Her fingers tightened along his back as he slid between her thighs, then higher, to lose himself within her.

Heaven, Alex knew with absolute certainty, would be this. Always this. With Olivia.

They made love. When he would have slowed down, to prolong the joining, she urged him with her hands, urged him deeper, which was how he wanted it. Hard and fast.

When they'd finished, their breathing slow enough to speak, neither appeared to miss the words of love that lay unspoken. Instead, both were content. Somehow the passion had seemed expression enough.

LATER, after Alex had taken Olivia home and returned to his unmade bed, he realized how empty his home felt. He removed his clothes once more and crawled into bed. Her perfume lingered again on the pillowcase and he wanted her so badly that he ached.

But what did he really want? Having Olivia meant accepting three children, too. There was no getting around that. Alex remembered the golf day. He'd tried—and hadn't done too badly, he'd come to realize.

If this was love—Alex turned onto his stomach and gripped the pillow—and he wasn't sure it was, though it must be pretty damn close—then the next step was something more . . . permanent.

He groaned. Would Olivia eventually want more than he could give or would an affair, even a long-term one, be enough for her? The real question was, would it be enough for him? He doubted it. The house already felt like a tomb. He knew she'd never let him stay at hers and, he had to face it, that was where all the fun was.

Because Olivia was there.

So, he had to decide if he was going to accept the whole family or give up the woman. And he'd better make up his mind before this thing went any further.

"OLIVIA? Telephone for you." Mary, the new assistant Judd had hired for the duration of tax season, held out the receiver.

"Thanks." Olivia swiveled her chair away from the computer terminal and took the receiver.

"Hello, Olivia Bennett speaking."

"Good. I've been waiting to hear your voice."

She recognized Alex's drawl right away. "Oh, hi. What do you need?"

"You."

She smiled into the receiver and caught Mary's curious look. She shrugged and picked up a pencil to fiddle with. "I can't help you with that right now. Is there anything else?"

"I need dinner tonight."

She mentally counted the number of chicken breasts she'd put into a pan this morning. There were enough for Alex to join them for dinner. "Okay, come over. We're having chicken."

"Let me take you out."

"On a Wednesday?"

"I can't wait until Friday. Let's go sit in a booth at the 108 House and eat hamburgers and talk about the weekend."

"What weekend?"

"The one coming up, where you and I head to my place and . . . watch movies."

"I'd like to, uh, watch movies with you, but Wolf has a game Friday."

"We'll go to the game and then we'll come back to my place."

"Let's talk about it tonight."

"Good. I'll pick you up at six-thirty."

"Okay." Olivia hung up the phone and returned to her work at the keyboard. She wondered if her life would ever slow down. She knew after April 15 she would have something of a break at work—not exactly a full-fledged vacation, but at least a lot of the pressure would be off. Some nights her elbow ached from the constant lifting of the lid of the copier. Copying, stapling, mailing filled her days, plus dealing with the million other things that arose in the office. Judd had hired someone to copy papers at night and Mary, who answered the phone, but Olivia was the one who answered everyone's questions and reported to Judd. Having Alex as a lover complicated her life in such a lovely way, though. Somehow there was always time for him.

Judd dropped a batch of papers onto her desk. "What's the smile for?"

Olivia realized she'd been grinning like an idiot. "Nothing much."

"Yeah, right. How's Alex?"

"Fine."

"Tell him we'll have to catch up on our racquetball games after tax season."

"I will." Judd leaned against the desk and Olivia gave up trying to enter the row of numbers into the computer. She swiveled her chair toward her boss. "Anything else?"

"Well . . ." He stalled until Mary left the room with an armload of papers to file. "Well," he began again, then cleared his throat. "Just be careful. You don't know how, uh, guys are."

Except for having been married to one, given birth to two and now working for an odd assortment of the species. "How are 'guys,' Judd?"

"Goofy," he answered, straightening to make an exit from a conversation, he was obviously uncomfortable with. "Guys are goofy."

"Well," Olivia said, watching Judd hurry from the room. "You won't get any arguments from me."

SHE REMEMBERED Judd's peculiar pronouncement on Saturday afternoon, when Alex and Wolf came downstairs to the workroom. She smiled a greeting, finished painting the petals of a purple flower earring and stuck it into an egg carton to dry.

Wolf planted himself in front of the card table and looked pleased with himself. "Hey, Mom, guess what!"

Olivia smiled at her son's animated expression. "What?"

"Alex said I could try driving his car."

She looked at Alex, who stuck his hands into his jeans pockets. "The GHI?"

"GTSI," he corrected.

"Whatever." The men exchanged looks and smiled at her.

"We won't be gone long. An hour, maybe." Wolf stepped back.

"Wait a minute," Olivia cautioned, standing up. She didn't like being towered over. It made her feel out of control. "I don't think you should be driving a fancy race car like that."

"Sports car, Olivia," Alex corrected. "And I'll be with him."

Olivia ignored him. "It doesn't even have a speedometer on it—just a bunch of other numbers. How do you know how fast you're going?"

Wolf sighed. "You can just . . . tell. Come on, Mom, it'll be okay."

"No."

"No?" two deep voices chorused.

"No," she repeated.

When Wolf would have protested, Alex interrupted him. "Okay, you're the boss. We'll just take it for a spin around Narragansett. I'll drive," he promised, stepping closer to give her a quick kiss before she could say anything else.

"Can we stop at the pier?"

"Sure," Alex said, winking at Olivia. "I always swing past the seawall and check out the girls."

"Great," the teenager said, sounding relieved. "What kind of sound system do you have?"

"Bring a couple of CDs and try it out," Alex said.

"Have a good time," Olivia called after them, relieved that Wolf had accepted Alex's presence in the family. Still, she knew she shouldn't fall too hard for Alex. He loved the challenge of a new product and the excitement of a new affair. Was that fair? She wasn't sure, but the man made love to her as if she was the only woman on earth. It was impossible to resist a man who looked at her with such passion, who touched her with such tender skill.

Olivia picked up another flower to paint. She'd enjoy the affair while it lasted, she promised herself. And she'd try not to fall in love with him any more than she had already.

9

THE NEXT WEEK was the busiest Olivia had ever known. Thanks to Alex, orders for Glitter Girl kits began to trickle in. The numbers on the invoices were higher than Olivia had ever dreamed. Nancy posed for the picture for the front of the box and the package began to look real.

Still, most of the decisions were left to Olivia, although Alex would give his opinion when asked. And he took his role as partner seriously enough to count rhinestones and staple plastic bags with the rest of the family.

Every extra minute was spent putting kits together. The boxes arrived late, but the cover turned out be exactly what Alex had envisioned and the board of directors approved. Even Nancy was pleased and took an empty box to school to show her fifth-grade classmates.

By the middle of March damp shreds of winter remained, but Olivia's spirits were rising. Income tax season was almost over. She planned to take a few days off in early May, as soon as the office settled down to its pre-tax season calm. Until then it was late nights and mornings that started too early.

"Mom, wake up!"

Olivia was too busy driving her lemon-yellow Cadillac along Route 95 to open her eyes. "Hmm." That meant *go away.*

"Mom." Nancy's voice grew louder. "I brought your coffee."

The highway turned into a diner. A waitress dressed in mint green handed her a silver plate piled high with chocolate-covered doughnuts. "Hmm?"

"Coffee," Josh called. "It's Saturday, remember?"

Olivia wrestled to wake up and wondered what she was supposed to remember. She shoved her pillow against the headboard and leaned back. She opened her eyes and attempted to smile as Nancy handed her a mug of coffee.

"Thanks," was all she managed to say.

Nancy sat down on the bed and frowned at her. "Don't you remember? We're s'posed to pack boxes this morning so we can take the rest of the weekend off."

Olivia stared at her coffee. It was all coming back to her. She'd stayed up late, trying to get a few extra things assembled so that the work wouldn't be overwhelming today. Everyone needed time off for good behavior. "Where's Wolf?"

Josh sat down on the bed too. He yawned. "He had SATs today," he said sleepily. "He told me to tell you that he should be back by noon."

"What time is it?"

"Nine."

Olivia groaned. "Oh, no! I have to get up before Alex gets here."

Josh grinned. "Too late. He's already here."

Nancy bounced on the bed. "Yeah, who do you think made the coffee?"

"I thought Wolf did."

"He made one pot, but Alex dumped it down the sink."

Olivia took a sip. The coffee was superb. "Where is he now?"

"Making breakfast."

"I didn't think he could cook."

Josh shrugged. "Well, he looks like he knows what he's doing." He leaned closer and whispered, "What's going on, Mom? You two are always smiling at each other."

Nancy nodded. "Yeah. And you go out together, too."

Olivia hesitated, swallowed a large mouthful of coffee and looked at her children. "Well, I'm not sure what to tell you. Alex and I enjoy being together—and we like working together."

"Except when you fight."

"We don't always agree on what's best for Glitter Girl, but that's the way business is. He gives me his opinion and I give him mine."

"I'll say," John added. "Everybody sure has a lot of opinions around here."

"No kidding," Nancy muttered. "I want to know if it's serious."

"Serious?"

"Like, is he gonna move in here? Audrey's mom got a boyfriend, and pretty soon he moved in with them and they had to watch football all the time, even when a better show was on."

"I don't think you have to worry about the television schedule," Olivia said, trying not to laugh.

"Well, is he moving in?"

"Of course not!"

"He's not?" Josh looked disappointed.

"Alex has a very nice house of his own," she assured them. "Why would he want to move in here?"

"Then it's not serious," Josh said.

"What's not serious?" Alex said from the hall. Without waiting for an answer, he called, "Olivia, are you decent? I brought you breakfast."

"Yeah, come in," Nancy said, answering for her mother. "She doesn't look too bad."

"Thanks," Olivia said, smoothing her hair and arranging the sheets around her chest.

"Morning," he said, looking gorgeous in jeans and a striped blue shirt and carrying a tray laden with plates. "I made the only thing I know how—cheese omelets and toast." He set down the tray in front of her. "We can all share."

"It looks wonderful." It also looked as if it would feed ten hungry Marines. The egg concoction stood about an inch high and the sides spilled over the plate and onto the tray.

"Let me cut it up." Alex reached for a knife and started to divide the enormous creation. "Here," he said, handing a plate with an omelet wedge and a piece of toast to Olivia. "I hope you like it."

"Thank you." Olivia hoped she'd like it, too. Especially since there was so much of it. "It smells good." She selected a fork and took a bite.

"Well?" Alex looked quite pleased with himself, as if he knew he deserved rave reviews. Olivia realized he'd probably made omelets for dozens of women "the morning after," then dismissed the thought. She was just grumpy because she'd been forced to wake up.

"It's very good," she managed to say. "I'm sure you've had lots of practice." Her jealousy surprised her, but then she'd never been tolerant of Jack's flirtations, either. And look what had happened—he'd run off to the Rockies with a redhead.

Alex shot her a speculative look. "I'll take that as a compliment, until I find out what you're talking about."

She smiled, sorry for the flash of feeling. "You make a great cup of coffee, too."

"I'm going to teach your oldest son how," he said, stabbing his own serving of omelet. Josh and Nancy left the room.

"I'm sorry I wasn't ready for work today. I slept late."

"You worked late. Josh told me."

"There was a lot to do."

"I know, but working yourself to death isn't going to help Glitter Girl."

"But there's so much at stake."

Alex smiled and Olivia's heart melted. "Finish your breakfast," he ordered. "There's nothing that can't wait a while longer. Josh and I are going to go over some numbers, Nancy's counting stones and watching cartoons, so you can take your time drinking your coffee." He stood up and winked at her. "We'll make do without you for a while longer."

"You will?"

"Of course."

Olivia watched as he left the room and shut the door behind him. When had Alex turned into a family man? And how long would it last?

THAT WAS POLLY'S QUESTION. "How long do you think this can last?" were her exact words four hours later.

"Shh," Olivia warned, looking toward the closed basement door. "He's downstairs."

"I don't care where he is." Her friend was fuming. "I just want to know what he's doing."

"What *we're* doing," Olivia said, picking up the leftover sandwiches from the dining room table. "It's not like he's the Big Bad Wolf and I'm a helpless virgin." Polly followed her into the narrow kitchen and helped herself to a cup of coffee. "That's hours old. I'll make a fresh pot."

Polly shook her head. "Don't bother. You know I'm not fussy about coffee." She took a sip to prove her point. "So, what are you—*plural*—doing?"

"Enjoying ourselves," Olivia said, pulling a length of plastic wrap from its box. "Very much."

"Uh-oh."

"What's that supposed to mean?"

"Sex, right?"

"Right." She lifted her chin. "I'm a grown-up."

"True."

"I don't have to defend myself."

"True, too." Polly looked offended. "I'm not acting like your conscience, for heaven's sake. I think it's great—have a wonderful time. Just as long as you don't get hurt."

"I'm not going to get hurt." *Because I've protected my heart every step of the way. At least, as much as I can.*

"He's sexy and gorgeous, Olivia. And you have him. Which I predicted, remember?" Polly didn't wait for an answer. "But what are you going to do now?"

Olivia put the platter into the refrigerator and shot her friend a wicked grin. "Enjoy him?"

Polly giggled. "Now *that's* the right attitude."

Olivia turned away to open the dishwasher and load the dirty breakfast dishes. She'd meant what she said. She would enjoy this time with Alex—this delirious, passionate, exciting and happy time—and no one would ever know how much she'd hurt when he moved on to a less complicated relationship. For move on he would. Men like Alex didn't stick around.

OLIVIA FASTENED her seat belt and rubbed the frost from the car window to peer at her house. "I'm not sure about this."

Alex started the engine and let the motor warm. "It'll be fine."

"I don't know. I don't feel right about leaving Wolf and Becky alone in the house."

"They're not alone."

"Just because Josh and Nancy are there doesn't mean anything," she said, giving him a worried look. "You don't know teenagers."

He eased the car onto the street and headed toward Route 1. "Sure I do. I was one, remember?"

Olivia waited until they'd reached the highway before answering. "I didn't know you then, but if you had your girlfriend over to the house for the evening, would you get rid of your brother and sister so you could, mmm, have privacy in the living room?"

Alex thought about it for a few minutes, but Olivia didn't mind the quiet. There were a few cars on the road, despite the fact that it was Saturday night. The cold weather must be keeping everyone indoors.

Though it was already March 14, Olivia was glad she'd worn her thickest sweater over the calf-length black skirt.

"No," he said finally.

Olivia felt a stab of relief. "Good."

"I'd pay them to leave me alone and I'd take my girlfriend into my bedroom and lock the door."

Olivia groaned and leaned back against the leather upholstery.

"I'm sure we'd just listen to music," he protested. "But it would be private. And speaking of privacy, here we are." He parked the car in the driveway and shut off the engine. Then he smiled at Olivia. "Now this is the best part of the day. It was tempting to climb into bed with you this morning. You looked so sleepy and so beautiful."

She smiled. "And the bed was so crowded."

"I noticed that. I couldn't come up with a plan to get you alone for an hour."

"Until now."

"Yes." He smiled and leaned forward to plant a kiss upon her lips. "Until now. How fast can you get your clothes off?"

"In the car?"

"No. The race starts as soon as I unlock the door. The first one who hits the bed stark naked wins."

She pretended to give the matter some thought. "What do I get if I win?"

He undid the buttons on her coat and slid his hand inside. "Anything you want," he said, cupping her breast.

Olivia tucked her arms around him. "And what if you win?"

"We stay in the car next time."

Olivia eyed the Ferrari's small interior. "I don't think it's possible to make love in this car, do you?"

"Maybe not, but I've always wanted to try." He began to slip her coat from her shoulders, but Olivia pulled him toward her.

"Not so fast," she whispered, kissing him. His lips were cool, his mouth warm. He slid closer to her on the leather seat and slid one warm hand underneath her sweater.

"Slower?" he asked. "Like this?"

Olivia inhaled as he moved his hand upward, pressing his thumb into the side of her breast with agonizing tenderness. His ability to turn her to jelly still surprised her. She lifted her lips from his and said, "I think we'd better go inside."

Alex slipped his hand inside her bra to cup her warm flesh. "Maybe you're right." He grinned at her in the darkness. "The windows are fogging up." He reluctantly slid his hand away and pulled her sweater down to her waist. "You have to admit that it's fun in the car."

"Uh, yes." *Fun* didn't begin to describe the sensation. Olivia wondered if her knees would carry her to the doorstep. "You're very good at this."

He raised one eyebrow. "My high school days are coming back to me. Of course, there was more room in the front seat of my mother's Ford."

"I'll bet." Olivia briefly considered what her own Buick must have been through with Wolf and Becky, then banished the uncomfortable thought from her mind.

"The best part," he mused, touching her knee, "was the leg."

Olivia looked at him, but he was looking at her knees. "Really?"

"Uh-huh. Skirts were—are—my favorite."

She had to ask, although she was beginning to have a pretty good idea what he was up to. "I probably should know better, but why are skirts your favorite?"

He pulled the hem of her skirt higher, inched his hand under the soft woolen material and slowly, deliberately, touched the bare skin of her thigh. "This is why," he murmured, his fingers exploring higher.

"Now I'm beginning to understand," she replied, her arms still around his neck. She leaned forward and kissed the patch of skin above his collar.

"Pay attention," he murmured. "This is the most important part."

"I'm all yours."

His hand moved on until he touched lace. "Nice," he said, running his fingers along the textured fabric. "What color?"

"Black."

She was warm and soft and he wanted to touch her until she forgot where she was. He urged her closer and she came willingly, pressing against his leg's hard length as Alex found her mouth in the darkness. He slid one finger under the elastic touching her bare skin, then urged the scrap of fabric aside to allow his fingers free access to the soft heat between her thighs.

"See?" he said, lifting his lips from hers. "I told you this was the best part."

"I'm not arguing," she replied, loving the intimate touch of his fingers, but wanting more. He kissed her again, and she opened her lips for his kiss while his fingers found her most intimate places and lingered with loving touches.

"Come here," he whispered, slipping his hand from her. He moved to her seat and tugged her onto his lap to face him. She straddled him, skirt at her hips, while Alex unzipped his slacks.

She wrapped her arms around his neck and smiled at him. "Alex, we could go inside and—"

"Ruin every fantasy I ever had about this car," he finished for her.

"I guess that wouldn't be very nice of me, would it?" She kissed her way along his chin, his jaw, lingered at his earlobe and nuzzled his neck.

He ran his hands up her thighs to her waist, pulling the silky fabric of her briefs to her hips. "Wait," she said, "I'll take them off."

But he held her still. "No room," he muttered. Olivia heard the fabric rip, but before she could protest, Alex placed himself against her and urged her down to slide over him and capture him in her tight warmth. He gasped, holding her still while he filled her.

She moved slightly, lifting herself, then filling herself again. She rested her head against his shoulder. "Looks like you won, after all," Olivia whispered.

He could see her breath in the cold night air, but the windows had fogged completely, giving them privacy despite the fact that they were parked in a driveway in the center of a neighborhood. She made love to him until he gripped her waist and felt her tighten once more around them, felt the trembling aftershocks of her climax as he, with a final thrust, exploded into her and felt his own world spin out of control.

Later, in the snug warmth of his living room, he waited for Olivia to finish taking a shower. Alex played the scene in his car and wondered what the hell had gotten into him. He normally had more manners than he'd displayed this evening.

He'd torn her silk underpants off her body in an uncharacteristic display of lust. The woman was dangerous, that was certain. She had no idea what she did to him, the way she shattered his self-control. He pulled the pieces of black silk from his pocket and frowned at them.

"What's wrong?" Olivia said, moving silently across the carpeted room.

Alex quickly shoved the evidence into his pocket. "Nothing."

"You looked so serious," she said, touching his face in a gesture of concern.

He smiled and kissed her fingers. "I was just thinking about getting a bigger car."

"I don't know," she whispered. "There's a lot to be said for a Ferrari 306 GST."

"308 GTSI," he corrected.

"Whatever," she said, downgrading the importance of a few letters as she stood on tiptoe to touch his lips with hers. "I liked the atmosphere."

Alex looked into her gorgeous blue eyes and smiled. "That's one way to put it. Atmosphere."

"What would you call it?"

"Out of control," he murmured, slipping his hand through her soft yellow curls and cupping the back of her head. "I always want you, do you know that?"

She shook her head. "No."

"It's true. I see you. I want you. It's that simple."

"I don't think anything is that simple, Alex."

"This is." He bent his head and touched her lips in a gentle kiss. "It can't be any other way."

BACK TO BUSINESS, Olivia decided on Monday morning. This week she would devote to tax season and Glitter Girl. Her love life with Alexander Leeds would be ignored, or at least put aside while normality took over.

Back to business, Alex told himself. There were phone calls to return, letters to answer and several day trips to Connecticut and Massachusetts to check on clients' products. Glitter Girl had taken up most of his attention—especially since he had invested in the company—but it was time to step back and take care of the rest of his life.

Easier said than done.

"When do I get to meet Mrs. Glitter Girl?" Paula dropped a stack of mail upon Alex's desk.

Alex shrugged. "One of these days."

"Never known you to be so mysterious," she mumbled, turning away from him. "You're not sending flowers, either. Why not?"

"I don't know. Guess there's not much need to send flowers." *How do you send flowers to someone you see almost every day?*

"I'll tell you why," she said, turning around and pointing a finger at him. "You send flowers when you're trying to impress a woman or when you're breaking it off. Nicely, of course. Whoever Mrs. Glitter is, she must be something special for you to be spending so much time with her."

"She is," he said, tapping his pen on the gray blotter. That was the difference, he realized. To Olivia he gave other kinds of gifts—useful ones, like food and time and caring.

Which was what she gave him, what he missed every day he wasn't with her.

To hell with it, Alex decided, and reached for the phone. He needed to hear Olivia's voice. Paula gave him a mock salute and headed out the door, closing it quietly behind her.

"South County Accountants," a woman's voice trilled. "Good afternoon."

"May I speak to Mrs. Bennett, please?"

"She's not at her desk right now. Would you like to leave a message?"

Alex frowned and swiveled around in his chair to face the window. No snow, but the trees were moving in the wind. "Thank you. Tell her Alex Leeds called and would like her to call when she has a moment."

"I'll do that. Thank you for calling."

Alex hung up the telephone, frustrated by the woman's cheerfulness. He didn't want polite phrases; he wanted to hear Olivia's voice on the other end of the line.

Mary caught Olivia when she returned from making bank deposits for Judd. "An Alex Leeds called, and wants you to call him back."

"Alex?" Olivia took the pink slip of paper with the message and double-checked the name. She hoped there was nothing wrong with Glitter Girl. She was determined to get through the week without the distraction of Alex blocking her progress. Not that he blocked anything, she thought, not being in love did put a person in a fog, even when it was the middle of tax season and you worked for a hyperactive tax accountant. A woman needed all the brains she could muster to concentrate on the work to be done just between the hours of nine and five.

Still, she couldn't wait to call Alex and hear his voice. As long as nothing was wrong, it would be the highlight of the day.

"I NEVER THOUGHT this was something you'd enjoy," Olivia said as they entered the high school auditorium. "The junior class talent show isn't exactly Broadway."

"Are you calling me a snob?"

"No." She handed four tickets to the teenage usher, who exchanged them for bright blue programs. "I'm simply trying to warn you." She smiled at some of the parents, old acquaintances, as they made their way to a row of empty seats near the back of the downstairs section.

Josh hesitated. "I'm going to sit with my friends," he said. "Okay?"

"Sure. Look for us after the show's over."

Olivia took off her heavy coat and arranged it behind her on the back of the seat. She sat down between Alex and Nancy and watched; parents and grandparents continued to fill the noisy auditorium.

Alex looked briefly at the program. "This is an annual thing, right?"

"Yes. I don't know how long ago it started, but I remember doing it when I went to school here."

"What does Wolf do?"

"I haven't any idea. He's been spending every afternoon and evening at rehearsals, but he wouldn't tell me
what act he was in."

"There are certainly a lot of people here tonight."

"It's traditionally the night for parents, but—" Olivia stopped. This was the first time she'd attended a
school function in the company of a man since Jack had
left.

"But?" Alex urged.

"Mmm, tomorrow the seniors fill this place and
heckle. I think the jokes tomorrow night are aimed
more at the seniors." Olivia scanned the program. "I
hope they keep it clean. Wolf warned me."

Alex surveyed the people around them. "The class
must make a small fortune on this."

"Wolf told me I couldn't come on Saturday or I'd
embarrass him. Looks like a lot of other parents were
told the same thing."

Nancy squirmed in her seat. "There's nobody I know
here. Can I buy popcorn?"

"No." Olivia looked at her watch. "It's after seven-
thirty. The show should be starting any minute now."

As if on cue, the auditorium lights dimmed and the
stage lights illuminated the curtain. Two students
dressed as cheerleaders came from the sides of the stage
to begin the series of skits that made up the show.

Alex stretched one arm over the back of Olivia's
chair, his fingers resting lightly on her shoulder. Comfortable, Olivia decided, and definitely distracting
enough to prevent her from hearing half of what was
happening on stage. She and Alex looked like a couple
to anyone who didn't know better. But what were they

really? Olivia clasped her hands in order to keep from grabbing Alex and telling him how much she loved him.

"Relax," he whispered close to her ear. "He'll do fine."

Men didn't have a clue sometimes, she decided, making a conscious effort to relax her hands. "You're right," she whispered back, hoping he'd think he'd offered the comforting words she needed to hear. *I love you* would have been a good start.

Wolf sauntered onto the stage dressed as a mermaid, and Olivia held her breath. Four of his friends, each garbed in fish costumes, gathered around to sing a song from the movie, *The Little Mermaid.*

"This is so awesome!" Nancy squealed and the crowd started laughing.

"A star is born," Olivia murmured.

Alex chuckled and shook his head as if he couldn't believe what he was seeing. "That kid has balls," he announced.

Nancy leaned forward and shook her head. "They're *fins*, Uncle Alex."

"Sorry," he said, clearly trying to hide a smile. "I never saw the movie."

Olivia frowned at him, then started laughing again; the teenagers on stage had begun to dance. When the song was over, Olivia burst into applause. "I can't believe he did that! No wonder he didn't want to tell me ahead of time!"

Alex squeezed her shoulder. "I can't wait to give him a hard time about it."

"Don't. He looked so serious."

"That was fear," Alex stated emphatically. "And right now he's backstage, happier than he's ever been because the skit is over."

"Think so?"

"Absolutely."

Later, when the show ended, Olivia and Alex waited at the back of the hall for Josh to appear, but it was Wolf who found them first.

"Well? What did you think?"

Olivia gave him a hug. "I didn't know you could sing."

"And I didn't know you had such talent," Alex said, offering his hand. Wolf took it and grinned.

"Me either. I was scared sh—uh, out of my mind."

"I'll bet," Nancy said. "That was pretty funny."

Wolf waved to someone behind Olivia. "Yeah. It was supposed to be." He turned back to his mother. "Is it all right if I go to Becky's house? She's having a bunch of kids back to celebrate."

"How will you get home?"

"I'll get a ride. Don't worry."

"Okay. Not too late, all right? We're planning to work all day."

He kissed her cheek. "Thanks, Mom. See you, everybody." With a wave he was off, heading for Becky Miller's side.

"He looks happy," Alex said, watching the group of kids talking together.

"She's a nice girl," Olivia said, "but I wish they weren't quite so serious about each other."

"There's nothing you can do to prevent anyone from falling in love," he said, helping her put her coat on.

"True," she agreed, stepping away from him to wave to Josh. *But there's a lot you can do to prevent getting hurt.* At least she hoped so.

"Come on," he said, catching up to her. "Let's go have dessert somewhere. My treat."

Olivia turned, and for a brief moment let herself believe that Alex Leeds would want to be part of her life forever. It was easier to imagine than she'd thought. "All of us?"

"Of course."

Olivia dared herself to hope. Just a little bit.

10

ALEX COULDN'T WAIT until Friday. Even though basketball season was over, he assumed Wolf would have a date. Josh was going to the movies with some kid named Brandon, and Nancy was going roller skating with the McCanns, according to information received from Olivia and confirmed by Judd.

Alex planned to spend those two hours surrounded by Olivia's sexy little body. Nothing could be more welcome. He'd been out of town. He'd heard her voice on the phone . . . maybe ten times. Somewhere in those phone calls a plan had been hatched to have the house to themselves.

"Why? It's easier to go to your place," Olivia had pointed out.

How could he explain his desire to be in her bed, in her room, in her house? Of course it didn't make any sense, but he wanted to. "I'm having it painted," he'd lied.

"You're lying."

"All right. I'm having it bombed for fleas."

"You don't have a dog."

"I'll get one," he'd promised. "Any kind you like."

"You're off the subject, Alex."

"Come on, sweetheart. We'll have the house to ourselves for once. An hour or two of mad, passionate lovemaking . . . how can you deny me?"

There'd been silence. "You're spoiled."

"That's a yes."

"I'll have to clean my room."

"No, you don't. Just don't turn the lights on. I'll never notice any dust." Dust had been absolutely the last thing on his mind.

"Promise?"

"Sure." He would have promised anything she'd asked. It was foolish, really, to want to be in her house with the children gone. He'd hung up the phone, walked out of the airport and driven straight to her house. It was seven o'clock and dark, and he'd been up since five o'clock three mornings in a row. He hated motel room beds and never slept well away from home. This time the room reminded him of Olivia and the trip to New York. It wasn't the same without her there beside him. Even room service had lost its appeal.

He yawned, trying to stay awake despite the back and forth motion of the windshield wipers clearing the drizzling sleet from the glass. The welcoming light over the front porch at Olivia's house looked better than anything he'd seen all week. He parked in front so he wouldn't block the driveway and saw Olivia open the front door and wave to him.

Alex hurried inside and slammed the door behind him. "Don't hug me," he said. "My coat is wet."

He was unreasonably disappointed when she followed his direction. "Here," she said instead, reaching for it. "I'll hang it by the stove."

"Thanks." The smell of pine and the warmth of the wood stove surrounded him; it was as if he'd finally arrived home—an odd feeling. He watched Olivia settle his coat onto a hook under the pine mantle. The living room was almost too warm, but the heat felt good. Water simmered on the stove top and the scent of orange peel filled the air.

She turned and smiled. "I missed you."

"It was a long week," he said, opening his arms; she came closer.

"But a profitable one?"

"Yes." He closed his arms around her, feeling her body ease against his in delightful ways. "For several clients, but especially for Glitter Girl."

She pulled back to study him and he could have looked into those blueberry eyes until April. "Really? How?"

He kissed her in answer, until she pulled away. "Guess I won't have your attention until I tell you."

She merely smiled. "That's right."

"You have a one-track mind," Alex noted, pretending to be aggravated. "I've always known that was one of your negative qualities."

"Oh, I have a lot of them," she said, reaching for his tie, Olivia began to undo the knot, then said, "But having a one-track mind is one of my better traits."

"Oh, really? How?"

"Well," she said, unbuttoning the top button of his shirt. "It gets me what I want. Almost as soon as I want it."

"And what do you want?" But Alex couldn't wait for an answer. He tugged her toward the couch so she could sit on his lap and continue to work on the buttons.

"Actually, Alex, you look absolutely exhausted. How was your trip, really?"

"It was business," he said, "just like every other trip." He leaned back against the couch and closed his eyes. "It's good to be back home."

"You should catch up on your rest tomorrow."

"No," he said, his eyes still closed. "Glitter Girl has a new distributor. I hired a rep for the Southeast region. He's a young kid—and hungry. Knows the market. I have a feeling we'll have more orders than we can handle."

"I love the sound of that. What's his name and how did you find him?" Olivia slipped off his lap and snuggled beside him. Alex stretched his legs in front of him and crossed his ankles.

Alex didn't answer. Olivia listened to the even sound of his breathing, then realized he'd fallen asleep. She didn't blame him. It was the kind of night to snuggle together on the couch. Her feet were cozy in purple socks, and she wore purple leggings and a pale lavender sweater to match the earrings she'd made herself. A new design, they dangled two inches from her earlobes and resembled flower petals woven together. She'd worked late on them the night before. Olivia snuggled into Alex's shoulder and curled up her feet beneath her. She'd just close her eyes for a minute, then she'd be fine.

"Hey, you guys! Wake up!"

Alex opened his eyes to see Nancy and Josh standing in front of him. For a second he didn't know where he was or why he was dreaming about Olivia's children, until he blinked twice and began to awaken. There was a heaviness on his right arm, and he looked down to see Olivia's golden hair spilled over his chest. He didn't want to wake her, but Nancy seemed determined to tell her mother about her evening.

"Chad was there, Mom. And Josh and Brandon came by and teased him and acted like jerks."

"I did not. Is there anything to eat?"

Olivia stirred and moved her head away from Alex's shoulder. He wanted to keep her against him, but didn't want to upset the kids. "Olivia?" he said. "Josh and Nancy are home."

"Oh, hi," she murmured, her voice sleepy. "Did you have a nice time?"

"I told you," Nancy said. "Josh was a jerk."

"But did you have fun?"

"Yeah," the girl said, leaning forward to give her mother a kiss on the cheek. "Lots."

"I'm glad." Olivia yawned. Nancy left the room. Olivia moved away from Alex and smiled ruefully. "I guess we didn't have our romantic evening."

"We still could, if you let me stay."

"No." Olivia knew what he meant, but didn't believe in having a man spend the night in her home. Not that Alex was just "a man," as if she had the opportunity every week to invite one to sleep over, but she didn't want her family's privacy invaded. And she didn't want to flaunt a sexual relationship in front of her children. "You know how I feel about that."

"I'm not just anyone," he said.

"Believe me, I know that. But . . ."

He didn't know why it was so important for him to stay. "I want to wake up in the morning with you beside me."

That's called marriage, Alex. Olivia shook her head.

"We got used to it in New York," he continued, his smile tempting. "Remember?"

She reached up and buttoned his shirt. "Of course I do. I liked that part, too."

"Then—"

"But this isn't New York and we're not in a hotel. There are other people to consider, so you have to go home."

Alex took her hand and kissed her palm. "You're right. I'm just cranky because I fell asleep and missed making love to you."

"You needed the rest more than you needed the . . . other."

He shook his head, his body hardening as he felt her warm thigh against his. "No, I need the 'other' very much."

"Tomorrow," she whispered, moving away from him to stand up. She went to get his coat and handed it to him. "Go home and get some rest."

"What about you?"

She looked at her watch. "It's almost ten. I'll wait up for Wolf."

"How is he? The romance with Becky still on?"

Olivia nodded. "The junior prom is in a couple of weeks and they're going together." She shook her head. "You wouldn't believe Wolf—he wanted to paint the Buick for the prom."

"Don't kids rent limos?"

"It's a fortune—believe me, I priced a couple of companies. It would work if they could find three other couples to share the cost, but Wolf says nobody's interested."

"That's a shame." Alex remembered the relief he'd felt when Judd's father had been coerced into loaning the boys his brand-new Cadillac for the senior prom. The two of them had picked up their dates as if they owned the world, or at least their part of Rhode Island. "A car is important."

"It's not the end of the world. Our car is fine if it's washed and waxed."

"But will it make it to the prom?"

"I had it tuned up," she said, snuggling back into his shoulder. "It's working better than ever."

Alex wanted to say more, but shut his mouth. The kid couldn't drive that Buick to a prom, for heaven's sake. "Let's have dinner tomorrow. An early dinner."

"Seven?"

"Not early enough," he said, listening to Nancy and Josh fighting over who had eaten the most brownies.

Olivia winced. "You're right," she said. "How about six?"

"Perfect." He kissed her quickly, not daring to linger. He knew how stubborn she was.

The ride home was dark and cold. So was his house. Alex didn't enjoy unpacking his suitcase in the solitude of his cold bedroom. He finally slid under the covers and picked up the remote control to scan forty-seven channels, relentless in his pursuit of quality television.

He wanted Olivia. He wanted to sleep with her, hold her, feed her, care for her, be part of the warmth and light that was her life. But he had to give in return, and that wasn't so easy. He'd have to bear responsibility for four lives, not just one. Live with four people, not one lover.

The thought terrified him. But not as much as it used to.

Alex settled on watching a hockey game, hoping a fight or two would break out and liven up the action. But he didn't watch it.

The time for a decision had arrived. Until now he'd avoided thoughts of commitment and marriage. Memories of his own parents' marriage and divorce still burned inside him. He'd vowed early on that he'd avoid the institution of marriage altogether—one sure way to avoid the painful aftermath of a failed relationship.

But Olivia deserved something better than a winter affair.

And maybe he did, too.

But, Alex worried, pressing the remote control and turning it to CNN to hear the news, how would he have to change his life? And was he capable of it?

Would he have to buy a station wagon?

He loved her—but how much? What was he willing to do about it? When it came right down to it, Alex knew, his heart sinking into his stomach, that was the most important question of all.

OLIVIA LOOKED AGAIN at the clock and the red digital numbers did little to calm her fears. Wolf was late. Not just late, but thirty-seven minutes late. Thirty-seven minutes weren't the end of the world, but because Wolf had never been late before, Olivia was worried.

She got out of bed and pulled on her robe and slippers. She couldn't stay in bed and stare at the wallpaper any longer. The bed was wide and empty, and she wished she'd let Alex stay with her. She needed him now—she would love to be held in those big arms again and be told that Wolf was fine.

Olivia went into the living room and put another log into the wood stove, poking the embers with a stick until flames flared red against the new wood. Once she was satisfied, she shut the door of the stove and went to the window to look outside. The neighbors across the street still had their lights on, but the rest of the street was dark. The driveway was empty, which made Olivia's stomach dance in nervous flutters. She crossed her arms over her chest and prayed that Wolf would pull up in the driveway this very second and tell her he was sorry he was late. She counted backward from one hundred, certain that when she reached "one" the Buick would be in sight.

It didn't work.

When she went into the kitchen, the clock said 12:30. One hour after Wolf's curfew. Should she call the police or the hospital? Should she find out if there was an accident? She picked up the phone to see if it was working, and a dial tone confirmed it was operating.

She held the receiver, wondering if she should call Becky's house. She hated to wake up the family at this hour if Wolf had left earlier. Maybe the kids had fallen asleep while watching a movie on the VCR.

Again she wished Alex was here. The heavy burden of handling everything alone swept over her, but what could she expect of Alex?

Comfort was the answer. She dialed his number, then hung up before it could ring. She had no right to bring him into this. He was her lover and her business partner—but he wasn't a husband. And she couldn't expect him to be.

Olivia heard a car engine and hurried through the dining room. A car door slammed and her son entered the living room as she reached the door.

"Sorry, Mom," he said.

Tears threatened to choke her. "Where have you been? Do you know what time it is?"

Wolf paled. "I got a ticket."

"What kind of ticket?"

He hesitated, then looked at her and replied, "A speeding ticket."

"Speeding?" Anger coursed through her and she tightened her hands into fists. The urge to hit him was strong. He hadn't had a spanking since he was very little, but she itched to give him one now. "Why on earth would you be speeding?"

"We were watching a movie at Becky's, and all of a sudden I realized what time it was and that I was late. So I hurried home."

"I've told you *never* to speed." Olivia tried not to raise her voice and wake the other children, but it wasn't easy. She shook with fury. "Haven't I told you that no matter how late you are, you're never to speed?"

He nodded, watching her with sad, dark eyes. "Yeah."

She crossed her arms in front of her and hugged her chest. "And?"

"Guess I didn't think."

"No, you certainly didn't." She watched as he pulled out his wallet and tossed his driver's license onto the dining room table.

"I'm sorry," he mumbled and turned away. He walked down the hall as if he had the weight of the world on his thin shoulders, then went upstairs to his room. Olivia swallowed the lump in her throat. Her son had scared her to death, but maybe she had been too hard on him. She didn't want his driver's license, but she did want to make sure he'd drive safely for the rest of his life.

She flicked the light switch and walked down the dark hall to her bedroom. For all of her self-sufficiency, she wished Alex were there. She could have used his strong support tonight.

Besides, she thought ruefully, padding into her room, her feet were cold.

"WHAT ARE YOU DOING?" Olivia asked, parking the Buick in the driveway and stepping out. Although there was nothing unusual about coming home from work to find Alex at her house, packaging Glitter Girl kits and having pizza delivered to the front door so she wouldn't have to cook, it *was* unusual to see Wolf sitting behind the wheel of the precious Ferrari.

"Nothing," Alex replied. Wolf opened his mouth and closed it, clearly looking to Alex to lead the conversation. They appeared too innocent.

"Is something wrong with the car?"

"It's not just a *car*, Mom." Wolf sighed. "It's an incredible piece of machinery that—"

"No, there's nothing," Alex said, cutting off Wolf's exposition. "How was your day?"

"Fine. Judd said to tell you to come by and pick up your tax returns anytime you want." She stepped closer, and the damp wind blew her hair off her face. Spring was on its way, but taking its time arriving in Rhode Island. "Isn't it too cold to be out here?"

"No," Wolf countered. "It's fine."

"You're right, Olivia." Alex took her arm and led her toward the front door. "We can talk inside."

Olivia knew something was up and had a feeling she wasn't going to approve. When had the two men in her life bonded together? For a man who didn't particularly enjoy children, Alex was doing all right with hers. She eyed them both with suspicion. Alex took her jacket and hung it up in the hall closet as if it were part of his everyday routine.

"Well?" she said, going into the kitchen. "Anybody want to tell me what's going on?" The two men—conspirators?—followed her. She opened the oven to make sure the timer had gone on as planned. A pot roast sizzled in a covered pan, so Olivia took a pot holder and lifted the lid to make certain there was plenty of juice surrounding the meat. Neither man spoke until she'd covered the roast again and closed the oven door.

"That smells good," Alex said. "I was going to order something, but Nancy said you had dinner already planned."

"We set the table," Wolf offered.

"Great." Olivia turned to lean against the counter. "So, what's up?"

"Do you remember the conversation we had about the prom?"

Olivia grew more baffled. "Not really."

"About Wolf driving the Buick."

She frowned, still trying to remember. "No."

"Well, anyway, it made me think." Alex paused. "I'd like to let Wolf drive the Ferrari to his prom."

"Are you out of your mind? Last week he got a speeding ticket, for heaven's sake. I just gave him his license back a few days ago."

"You don't have to talk about me like I'm not here," Wolf grumbled. "And I've learned my lesson. Alex has taught me how to drive his car safely and without breaking the speed limit."

"Oh, he has, has he?" She folded her arms in front of her and looked at Alex. "Don't I have a say in this—I mean, this being my family and my house and all?"

Alex looked surprised. "I thought it was a good idea. I thought you'd be pleased."

"That's a fast car, Alex. Anything could happen."

"Wolf knows it's not a toy."

Olivia nodded toward her son. "Wolf, you find some homework to do."

When they were alone in the small kitchen, Alex frowned and ran his fingers through his hair. "For heaven's sake, Olivia . . ."

"You should have talked to me first."

"I realize that now, but I thought it was a great idea. The kid shouldn't have to go to his junior prom driving that old piece of—"

"Watch it," she warned. "I've gone without a lot of things for Glitter Girl and a car is one of them."

"I'm not criticizing you, but that's my point. You've gone without a lot for the business, but why should Wolf have to go without, too? Here's a chance for him to drive a Ferrari, for heaven's sake."

Olivia was silent for a moment. "You're making a villain out of me. I don't like it."

"I apologize. I should have talked to you about it before I talked to him." Alex stepped closer and put his large hands upon her shoulders. "I honestly thought it would be one less thing for you to worry about."

She looked up at him, her blue eyes clouded with worry. "Is it safe for him to drive?"

"Yes." He wanted to say *Safer than the Buick*, but kept his mouth shut.

"But what if something happens, like someone backs into it in the parking lot at the Marriott? Aren't you taking a big risk?"

"I have a lot of insurance, and I'll give Wolf detailed instructions about parking. He's to treat that car like it was made of glass."

"I don't know about this, Alex. I'll have to think about it."

"Good enough. But do me a favor. Ask Judd what he drove to our senior prom, please."

"What does Judd have to do with this?" Olivia suspected this was in the 'guys are goofy' category.

"Just ask, okay?" Alex smiled, making himself look handsome and mysterious at the same time.

Olivia weakened, wishing every night found them together in the kitchen before dinner. "Sure." She lifted her lips for his kiss and held him close.

Later, when the dishes were clean and the house quiet, Olivia soaked in the bathtub and thought about her conversation with Alex. The man who swore he wanted nothing to do with working with kids was not only working with them, but playing with them, too.

And caring about them. That was growing more obvious every day. Why else would he consider lending his most precious possession to Wolf?

"NOT LIKE THAT. Tuck it in a smooth line."

"I can't do it."

"Hold still," Alex told the perspiring teenager. He carefully smoothed the white shirt.

"These pants are too big. They gave me the wrong size."

"No, they're adjustable." He showed Wolf the elastic inside of the waistband and adjusted the clips on each side of Wolf's waist. "Tell me when they're tight enough."

"I look like a geek."

"You're not used to it, that's all. Actually, you're going to look sophisticated."

"No, I look like a geek."

"Your mother is going to cry when she sees you. There, how's that?"

Wolf stuck his thumb into his waistband. "Yeah. That's good."

"Do your shirt again. Make sure it's tucked in tightly."

Wolf unzipped the black tuxedo pants and smoothed the white shirt along his abdomen, then fastened the pants. "Got it."

"Now for the cummerbund." Alex searched through the mess on Wolf's bed until he found the strip of emerald-green material. "Let me guess. Your date is wearing a green dress."

Wolf winced. "I wanted to wear red, but Mom said we'd look like a Christmas card."

"You're always safe matching," Alex agreed, hooking the cummerbund around Wolf's slender waist. "There."

Wolf looked down at his outfit. "I liked the red better."

"Fasten the neck on your shirt," Alex directed, finding the bow tie draped over the teenager's desk chair. "Turn around. We're almost there."

Wolf lifted his chin and Alex fixed the tie. "Who invented this stuff, anyway?"

"Cary Grant."

"Who?"

"Never mind. Bad joke." Alex stepped back and surveyed his work. "Last thing on is the jacket."

"I hung it up in the closet." Wolf walked gingerly to the closet and took out the black tuxedo jacket. "I hope this fits."

"Didn't you try it on in the store?"

"Yeah. A few weeks ago." He slipped on the coat. "But I already had to exchange the shoes because they were too big." He adjusted the cuffs and stood in front of Alex. "Well?"

Alex surveyed the tall young man, suddenly transformed into a much older, sophisticated version of Wolfgang Bennett. "Button the jacket and you're ready to go. You look great."

He did as instructed. "I'm so nervous."

"You should see your mother." *And I'm not exactly a robot myself.*

Wolf grinned. "She's been bugging me about the flowers and the Ferrari for weeks. Becky even gave me a clipping of her dress from *Seventeen* magazine so I'd have the right color, and Mom's been carrying it around like it was the recipe for making money or something."

Alex thought of Olivia's enthusiasm and grinned back. "She has gotten a little carried away."

"Yeah," Wolf agreed, grabbing his wallet and stuffing it into the inside pocket of his jacket. "You know how she is."

Yes, he thought, he knew exactly how Olivia was. Beautiful, warm, loving and independent. Exactly how she would always be, which was why he loved her. And why his decision tonight had become an easy one.

Well, not exactly easy, he amended, thinking of a few sleepless nights. *Inevitable* was a better word.

"Are you ready?" Olivia called through the closed door. "It's almost time to go and I want to get some pictures."

"Coming," Wolf called, then turned to Alex. "She's bought three rolls of film."

Alex chuckled. "You'd better get out there."

He followed the boy into the hall, then the living room where the rest of the family waited. It was warm for the second week of April; the living-room windows were open and a soft breeze brought the aroma of fresh earth, although the sky looked as if it could rain later.

Alex saw Olivia's eyes fill with tears and watched her blink them back before she spoke. "You look so handsome," she said, then paused. "I wish your father could see you right now."

"I thought I looked like your side of the family," Wolf teased, plainly refusing to be sentimental.

"Quit clowning around and stand over there by the front door." He did as he was told and made a face at Josh.

"Quit laughing, kid. This will be you in a few years." Josh shook his head. "No way."

Nancy took Wolf's arm and gazed upward with ad-oration. "You look absolutely, positively gorgeous," she gushed. "I can't wait to see Becky."

"Say cheese," Olivia said, readying the camera.

"Cheese." He waited and smiled while she snapped another picture. "C'mon, Mom...."

"Okay, now you, Alex and Josh, stand together and smile."

"Just the boys," Alex corrected, not budging from his spot by the door.

"Oh." She turned raised eyebrows in his direction. "You're not part of this prom project anymore?"

"Yeah," Wolf said. "You should go down in history as the man who loaned me a Ferrari." Alex shook his head, but joined the two Bennett boys. They tolerated several poses before Wolf lost patience.

"Mom, do we have to make a production out of this?"

Olivia studied the camera and advanced the film. "What do you mean?"

"Do you have to—?" he began, but Alex stepped between them and shot Wolf a warning look.

"I think it's time Wolf picked up his date," Alex interjected.

Olivia looked at her watch. "All right, we'll see you over there in—"

"Half an hour," her son supplied. "Everyone else is meeting there so the parents can take pictures."

"Great." Olivia stepped up to him and gave him a hug. "You do look absolutely gorgeous. Drive carefully, okay?"

"No, Mom, I'm going to be careless and weave all over the road."

She kissed his cheek. "Very funny. Don't forget the flowers."

"Here," Nancy said, handing him a white box. "I got 'em out of the refrigerator for you."

"Thanks." Wolf took the box, then raced back to his bedroom.

Alex stepped closer to Olivia and put a reassuring arm around her shoulder. "He's going to have a great time."

"I know," she sniffed, "but he looks so *old*." Wolf appeared carrying a brown paper bag. "My clothes for the post-prom at Riverbend," he explained.

"Riverbend?" Alex asked. "The health club?"

"Yeah. We've rented it from eleven to three. Pretty cool, huh? Then after that we're going to the beach to watch the sun rise."

"Just make sure you don't hit any potholes in the parking lot."

"I won't." He held out his hand to Alex. "Thanks a lot for loaning me the Ferrari. Becky can't believe it, and neither can any of the other guys."

"The keys are in the ignition. Just remember everything I taught you."

"I will."

Alex resisted the urge to stand at the window and watch Wolf get into the Ferrari. No one but Judd had ever driven his car until now, and he didn't know if he could watch a teenager drive it out of sight.

"You're a nice man," Olivia said, wrapping her arms around him. "I can't believe you did that."

He shrugged. "Just call me Uncle Alex."

She smiled. "Okay, Uncle Alex. Here's the plan, now that we're down to one car. I drop you off at your place and then I go take thirty or forty pictures of the kids, then I rent a couple of movies for Josh and Nancy, swing back here, drop them off and end up at your house."

He kissed her. "As long as you end up at my place I'm happy."

"Good." She picked up her purse, Josh handed her a list of acceptable movies, and Nancy raced out the door ahead of both of them.

Alex took a deep breath. He'd stood in as father this afternoon, and didn't think he'd done too badly. He whistled, despite having to sit in the front seat of the Buick while Olivia struggled to start the old beast. The engine finally came to life, and Olivia sighed with relief.

"Business is getting better, right?" she asked.

"Glitter Girl will be in the black before you know it," he assured her. "The only trouble we're going to have is keeping up with the orders."

"I feel that way already."

"Maybe Judd should start looking for a new secretary."

Olivia smiled and put the car into gear. "It's too soon to think that far ahead, but wouldn't that be fantastic?"

It would be fantastic, he thought, looking at the way her face lighted up, to wake up next to that smile every morning for the rest of his life.

11

ALEX HAD IT ALL figured out. He surveyed the room with satisfaction; located at the north end of the house, the den was an intimate room lined with bookshelves and, at the far end, a fieldstone fireplace. He'd built a small fire, and candles glowed from the pine shelf above the hearth.

Olivia had once said this was her favorite room.

When he heard her car pull into the driveway he took one more quick look around to make certain everything was in place, then hurried through the house. He heard Olivia knock twice before he reached the kitchen entry and opened the door.

Olivia made a face at him. "Hi. Where've you been?"

"At the other end of the house. Hi, yourself."

She looked at him with a curious expression. "What's up?"

Alex moved away so she could step inside. "Nothing. Why?"

"You had a strange look on your face, as if you didn't expect to see me." She glanced at her watch, then back at him. "Am I early?"

"No, of course not. I was just busy getting the house—never mind." Alex wondered when he had become so transparent. "Come on into the den. I have a fire going for us."

"It's sixty degrees out."

"It's going to rain. Besides, I thought it would be uh, cozier this way."

Olivia followed Alex into the den. Something was different about tonight. She'd sensed it the moment he'd opened the door. The music of Andrew Lloyd Webber played softly from the audio equipment in the pine bookcases by the window, and the aroma of burning apple wood filled the air.

She stopped just inside the door. "What's going on?"

He gave her a quick kiss on the mouth. "What do you mean?"

"'Music of the Night'?"

"I bought the CD a few days ago."

"Why the fire? It's April 11."

"I thought it would be more romantic."

"If it was any more romantic, we'd be going to the prom," Olivia muttered, unsettled by the feeling of mystery in the air. She tried to smile. "Maybe I should have dressed in something fancier than jeans."

Alex thought about kissing her again, but decided to continue with his plan. First they'd talk. After that would be a celebration dinner and lovemaking. If he could just get to the talking part, everything would fall into place. "You look fine, Olivia. Come on, I'll pour the wine, we can sit in front of the fireplace, and you can tell me how great I am at building a fire."

"All right." She curled up on the couch, tucking her legs underneath her. "Gee, Alex, what a beautiful fire." She grinned at him. "How was that?"

"Perfect, thank you. Wait here." Alex hurried into the kitchen for the wine he'd opened and kept in the refrigerator to chill. Not just any wine, but a *spumante* chosen especially for the occasion. So far, so good, except that Olivia didn't seem to understand that this was a romantic evening, and not just a casual Friday night dinner together. He'd have to turn up the heat.

"Comfortable?"

Olivia nodded. "Absolutely. I think I took some great pictures," she said, sounding pleased.

"Good."

"Becky looked gorgeous in a green and silver dress, and all the kids posed in front of a forsythia bush."

This mother was obviously not ready for romance. Alex decided he'd better let her get the prom out of her system before he went on to more serious matters. He handed her a glass of sparkling wine and resigned himself to hearing more about teenagers. "How many were there?"

"Four couples and several parents. I think Wolf was happy that I wasn't the only mother obsessed with recording the big event."

"Face it, Olivia. If the car had had a back seat, you'd have been it."

"I still can't get over the way Wolf looked in his tuxedo. He was so handsome."

"He didn't have any trouble with the car, did he?"

"Is that why you're so nervous?"

"What?"

"You've been acting like a man with other things on his mind."

"Well, as a matter of fact . . ."

"I understand," she said. "You were wonderful to let him borrow it. I'm glad you talked me into it. I hate to admit it, but Wolf looked like he'd been driving expensive cars all his life."

"We all do, once we get behind the wheel." He touched her glass with his. "What shall we toast to?"

"Young love?" she offered, thinking of Wolf and Becky.

Alex shook his head, and his green eyes were suddenly hooded; was it the firelight? "No."

"Success?"

He winced. "Not that either. How about—" his voice grew low and intimate, as if he were sharing an intimate joke "—to spring?"

"All right." She touched her glass to his in a symbolic gesture. "To the end of a long winter."

"And the beginning of a new season."

"I didn't know you liked spring so much."

"Oh, I do," he murmured, leaning forward to kiss her. "I do so much more than I've ever told you." His lips met hers in a kiss that started out light and quickly deepened into much more.

Alex lifted his head and moved away. He had to keep his mind on the plans for the evening. Rolling around on the couch was not on the priority list. "Olivia," he began, searching for the right words. "There's something . . ."

She peeled off her sweatshirt. "Sorry, Alex, but it's getting pretty warm in here."

Alex got up from the couch and opened the double windows a few inches. "There," he said, "That should help."

Olivia straightened her pink T-shirt and pushed her hair away from her face. She retrieved her glass and took a sip. "Guess I'm not used to the warm weather."

"Next week is Easter."

"And the week after that is spring vacation." She smiled. "Good thing I have a lot of work for the kids to do."

Alex began again. "Speaking of spring vacation . . ." He'd dreamed of an idea of spending the week in Florida, in an elegant condo in Disney World, where the Bennett children would be occupied with sightseeing while he occupied himself with Olivia. But he couldn't broach the subject without finding the romantic words to go with it, so he closed his mouth.

"I brought some figures for you to look at," Olivia resumed. "There's a price change on a few of the findings and I wondered if it was going to make any difference. And I also wondered if we should order more boxes or wait."

Alex drained his glass. He didn't want to start talking about business, but Olivia's questions were valid ones. "Let's talk about that tomorrow, when I have the figures in front of me," he suggested, hoping to head her off. He moved closer to her on the couch. "Olivia . . ."

She smiled at him and put her arms around his neck. "Mmm?"

He tried again. "Wait, sweetheart," but she drew near and sat on his lap.

"What, Alex?" she said, trailing little kisses along his ear. "Do you have spring fever?"

"Absolutely," he breathed, feeling his body begin to ache.

"Good." She bent her head to his, kissing him lightly. But when she would have pulled away he held her close, slanting his mouth across hers.

When at last they separated, Olivia raised her glass to her lips with a shaking hand. Once again Alex's caresses had changed her from a responsible mother to a one hundred percent melting female, and she loved every passionate minute. Between the heat of the fire and the wine, she hadn't had a chance to cool off. She leaned over to put down her glass.

"Don't wiggle like that."

He heard her soft laugh. "Why not?"

"You know why," Alex murmured, easing his hand up her shirt to cup her breast. "Despite spring fever, I have to finish cooking dinner."

"This is quite a role reversal. Are you sure you're feeling okay?"

"I don't know." Desire and nerves warred in his abdomen.

"Are you sick?"

Desire won. He reached between her breasts and unsnapped her brassiere. "Not anymore," he said, lifting up her shirt in one smooth motion. She was naked from the waist up.

"What about dinner?"

Alex pulled her still closer, so that his lips were inches from her breasts. "Forget dinner. You and I have more important things to do."

"Such as?" she whispered. Despite the barrier of denim, the straddling position was an oddly intimate one.

"Making love to each other," he answered before touching each nipple with his lips.

"Right here?"

His hands dropped to her jeans and unsnapped the waistband. "I don't think we have any other choice."

If Alex had expected an argument, he was wrong. "Sounds perfect," she murmured, reaching for his shirt. "Who gets to be on top?"

He grinned. "You decide."

"Well," Olivia drawled, sliding away from him in order to slip off her jeans and underwear. "I think we should finish what we started."

"I agree," he said, pulling off his shirt.

"Take off your pants," she said, smiling at him. "I've always wanted to say that to someone," she confessed.

"It's rather effective," he admitted, doing as instructed. "Although I don't think I've ever used those exact words myself."

"You haven't?"

Alex shook his head and grabbed Olivia's hand. "I'm tired of playing."

She followed him back onto the couch and straddled his lap once again. "So am I, Alex. What do you suggest we do next?"

"Come here," he ordered, sliding his hands along her buttocks and positioning her above him. "I have a lot of ideas."

Tight and warm and welcoming, she took him smoothly within her. Exactly where he wanted to be. She moved, stroking the length of him within her body, until Alex placed his hands upon her slim hips in order to slow her down before he totally lost control.

Balancing herself on his shoulders, she tightened her grip. They moved together in a slow and easy rhythm. Olivia wanted to make it last. She wanted him filling her so intimately, wanted to hold him inside her until the last possible moment.

There was something about spring, the promise of summer despite the weak sunlight and damp winds of a Rhode Island April, that made her want to hold on to her man and not let him go until they both dropped, exhausted and trembling, onto the cushions of the corduroy love seat.

"WELL, WHAT DO YOU THINK?"

"I love it," Olivia answered, taking another mouthful of the lasagna. "Did you make it yourself?"

Alex smiled; his plans were back on track. They'd made love once again in the bedroom an hour ago. Now it was after eleven. With luck he'd have the answer he wanted by midnight. "Paula, my secretary, made it for us. I've used her catering skills before."

"For seductive candlelight dinners?"

"No. For entertaining business clients." He looked her right in the eye. "Honest."

"I didn't say anything."

"You don't have to. Your face gives you away." It was the perfect opening for what he had to say. *Will you marry me?* should have been easy, but the question stuck in his throat like a huge piece of Italian bread. "More bread?" he stammered.

"No, thank you." She looked at him strangely. "Are you sure you're all right?"

"Of course. Why?"

"You've been acting odd all evening. I know it must be hard for you to think about a teenager driving your car. Like I said before, you're a nice man, Alex Leeds."

"Not so nice," he denied, remembering his seduction plans of just a few months ago. Had he really planned to ignore Olivia's children as if they didn't exist?

"Uncle Alex" had come a long way.

"I shouldn't stay much longer. I told the kids I'd be home by midnight, and I hate to leave them this long."

"They're probably thrilled to be watching movies."

She smiled. "Yes, you're right. But I—"

The phone rang shrilly from the kitchen wall. Damn. How would he ever say what he had to say?

"That's probably Josh now, wondering when I'm coming home."

"I'm going to drive you," he said, standing up. "I don't like the idea of you driving alone this late. We'll trade cars tomorrow." He took three steps into the kitchen and lifted the receiver. "Hello?"

"This is the South Kingstown Police, and I'm trying to reach a Mrs. Bennett."

"She's right here," Alex replied, feeling a sense of dread as he heard the tone of the officer's voice. "What is this about?"

"Her son—Josh, I think was the name—gave me this number. There's been an accident."

Olivia stepped into the kitchen, carrying the dinner plates and looking curiously at Alex. "What is it?" She stopped when she saw the expression on his face. "Alex?"

Alex held her gaze, but moved his lips to ask, "How bad is it?"

"I can't say for sure. Her son, the driver of the vehicle, has been taken by ambulance to South County Hospital. They'll need her there."

"We'll be there right away." Alex hung up the phone and reached for Olivia.

"What?" she said, her skin losing color. "Tell me."

"There's been an accident—" He never got to finish. The plates crashed to the brick floor, drowning his words.

OLIVIA DIDN'T KNOW how she got into the car. She didn't remember being driven to the hospital or being guided by Alex through the emergency doors. *Please let him be all right* kept running through her head.

Alex kept a hold on her arm as if he thought she'd fall to the floor in a heap. "I'm okay," she said, and attempted to pull away from his grip. She didn't want to act as though anything was wrong. She didn't want to think that Wolf was in such serious condition that she would fall to the floor when she heard the truth.

Alex let her go, and she moved away, pushing through another set of doors off the waiting room. She quickly approached the nurse behind the U-shaped counter. "I'm Mrs. Bennett. Where's my son?"

The nurse, a tall woman with short brown hair, looked sympathetic. "He's in an examining room," she replied, her voice soft. "The doctor is with him."

"Can I see him?"

"Not yet. I'll let you know as soon as you can, I promise."

"But I'm his mother. He needs me."

The woman shook her head. "Not right now, he doesn't. Believe me, the best thing you can do is to stay out of the doctor's way. Your son is being taken care of quite well."

"Is he—going to be all right?"

"The doctor will be out as soon as he can, Mrs. Bennett. I'm afraid I can't tell you anything else."

"What about Becky? She must have been in the car with him—"

"You'll have to talk to the police about the accident. I'm sorry, I can't tell you anything further." The nurse looked at Alex. "Mr. Bennett? Would you step over here and give us some medical information?"

Alex shook his head. "I'm a friend of the family."

"Mrs. Bennett? Please?" She had Olivia's attention again, she pointed to a cubicle to her right. "Have a seat. If you could just give us some information, please?"

Olivia stepped around the counter and sat down in a plastic chair while the nurse took a seat in front of a computer. She punched a few numbers and then began asking questions. Olivia struggled to remember her phone number, Wolf's social security number, and the name of her insurance company. The questions seemed endless, but answering them kept her from screaming.

Please let him be all right.

When the nurse had finished, Olivia closed her eyes, willing herself not to collapse into tears. The room smelled of antiseptic and the fluorescent lights hurt her eyes. She heard snatches of conversation behind the curtains. Two orderlies walked by, telling jokes. A policeman pushed open the double doors and strode to the counter.

"Any word on the teenager yet?"

The nurse took him aside and they spoke in quiet tones at the other side of the counter.

"Alex . . ." Olivia started to reach for him, but he walked away, heading for the policeman. She watched them talk for a long, anguished moment, then Alex returned to her side. He took her arm and helped her out of the chair.

"Come on," he said, "Let's go in the waiting room."

"But, Alex . . ."

"Come on, Olivia. We can talk there. They'll know where we are."

Olivia wanted to hit him. She had no intention of moving. She planned to stand in the middle of the emergency area until someone took her to see her son. She wanted Wolf to live.

Alex hauled her through the doors despite her protests. She didn't want to go anywhere and resented being taken out of the emergency room. When they were seated in the empty waiting area, Alex took Olivia's hands into his. "The policeman is a friend of mine. He told me that Wolf's unconscious. They're taking him for X-rays."

"X-rays of what?"

"His arm and—"

Her stomach muscles tightened. "And?"

"His neck." Olivia thought she was going to vomit, but willed herself to listen to what Alex was explaining. "Because he hit his head, the neck X-rays are a precaution. They don't want him to move until they make certain that nothing's broken."

"And Becky?"

"A little shaken up, but okay. Her parents picked her up a few minutes ago, even though she wanted to stay here and find out how Wolf—anyway, there's not a scratch on her, just a lot of glass in her hair. I guess they were heading to the post-prom in Peace Dale when the accident happened."

"Thank God she's all right." Olivia put her head between her hands and Alex put one arm around her shoulders. "That damn car. He had no business driving something like that."

"Olivia . . ."

"No," she said, pulling away from his embrace. "I never should have let the two of you talk me into it. I didn't follow my own instincts, and look what happened!"

Alex tried once more. "It's no one's fault, Olivia. It was the construction on Route 1. That and the rain. John, the policeman, explained. . . ."

"I don't want to hear any more." She stared at the closed doors. "I'm going to go see if they'll let me in."

Alex didn't try to stop her. He realized he couldn't, even if he'd wanted to. She had every right to see her son, to discover if he would live or die. He watched her push the double doors open and disappear.

The damn car. Alex wished he could take back the last few weeks. He'd failed Olivia, failed at fatherhood, failed the big time. He should have rented a limo for the kid, should have done anything but let him get behind the wheel of a fast car. What had ever made him think he could succeed at being a father?

Alex waited in the room until he couldn't sit still any longer. He thought he'd explode with fear. The clock edged toward midnight, and finally he stood up and went into the emergency room. The nurse looked up.

"Where's Mrs. Bennett?" he asked.

"With her son and the doctor." The woman smiled. "He's going to pull through—nothing's broken, and he's regained consciousness."

Alex's knees began to buckle, and he grabbed the counter for support. "Thank you," he managed to reply. "Thank you for everything."

"Are you okay? Maybe you should sit down."

"I'll be fine," he replied. The curtained areas were closed off, and Alex hesitated to intrude upon Olivia and Wolf. She'd made it clear she didn't need him right now. She needed to talk to the doctor more than she needed to talk to her lover.

Then he remembered the policeman's words on the phone. "Her son gave us this number," the man had said. Which meant Josh and Nancy must be aware that something was wrong.

Alex groaned. Josh must be worried sick. Hopefully Nancy was already asleep before the phone call came in. The poor kid would have no way of knowing what happened, even if he knew why the police needed to call his mother.

"I have to leave for a while," he told the nurse. "Could you tell Mrs. Bennett that I've gone—?"

The phone rang and she picked it up. "Emergency, Mrs. Venturini." She nodded to Alex. "I'll tell her," she said, then her attention was diverted to the phone call.

He waited until he had her attention once again. "Tell her I've gone home to the kids," he said. "Can you do that?"

"One moment," she said into the receiver, looked at Alex and smiled. "Yes, fine. Go home and get some rest."

Rest was the last thing he needed, Alex knew, but he nodded and left the hospital. He had one moment of panic when he reached into his pants pocket and didn't feel the car keys. He stopped in the middle of the parking lot, enclosed in a whirl of mist, then found his way toward the Buick. Luckily the keys were hanging from the ignition.

"Alex," a voice said behind him. He turned, to see the policeman who had been in the emergency room earlier.

"Thanks for your help tonight, John. I appreciate it."

"I just wanted you to know that your car will be towed out of there, hopefully by morning. You can call the station and find out where it is."

"Thanks." The Ferrari was the last of his worries right now. Alex opened the Buick's door and realized that by taking the car he was stranding Olivia at the hospital without transportation. He turned back to the policeman. "Could you give me a lift to Matunuck? I need to leave Mrs. Bennett's car here."

"Sure, if you don't mind riding in the back."

"No problem," Alex said, closing the car door. He'd be home within ten minutes. That was all that counted.

12

"EVERYTHING'S ALL RIGHT," Alex said, hurrying to reassure Nancy and Josh as he approached the open front door where they stood waiting, clearly scared. "Wolf's going to be okay." Two more steps brought him to the children, then they surrounded him and held on.

He'd thought he'd be awkward, inexperienced as he was at comforting kids. But it was the most natural thing in the world to put his arms around Olivia's two children and hold them tightly against him before kicking the door shut to keep out the damp night air.

Josh lifted his head, his gaze serious behind the glasses. "What happened? Where's Mom? Where's Wolf?"

"Come on." Alex tugged Nancy with him toward the old sofa. "Sit down and I'll tell you all about it."

"But Wolf—" Nancy started, almost choking.

"Is going to be fine," Alex finished for the little girl.

"He is? Really?"

"I promise, Nancy. The doctor told us so."

"But where's Mom?"

"Does Wolf have to stay in the hospital?"

Alex sat down on the old sofa and the children joined him there. Every light in the house was on, he noted. "They're both still at the hospital. Wolf had an accident with the car coming home from the prom, so he and Becky were taken to South County Hospital." He tightened his hold on the children. "Wolf had to have X-rays, but he's going to be okay. It's just going to take some time before your mother can bring him home."

Nancy began weeping softly, huge, fat tears running down her face. "I want Mom," she cried. "I really do."

"I know, sweetheart," Alex said, hugging her. "She'll be home as soon as she can, I promise."

"Really?"

Alex nodded. "Really." He turned to Josh, who sat quietly to his right. "Josh? Are you okay?"

"When the police called," he said in a low voice, "I was never so scared in my whole life."

Alex knew exactly how the boy had felt. "I can understand that."

"You can?"

"Yeah. I was pretty scared myself for a while." Alex remembered the smell of the hospital as he'd gripped Olivia's arm. "And so was your mother. Until the nurse told me Wolf was going to be okay."

"What's the matter with him?"

"He got a pretty nasty bump on the head and hurt his neck."

"What about Becky? She didn't . . . die, did she?"

"No, honey," he said, putting his arm around the little girl. "She's fine. In fact, she went home from the hospital already."

Nancy yawned and snuggled against Alex. "It's really late, isn't it?"

"Were you watching movies all this time?"

"No. I went to bed 'cause Josh wanted to watch *Terminator* 2 again."

"It's my favorite!" he protested.

Nancy ignored her brother. "Then the phone rang and woke me up. I thought it was gonna be Mom."

Alex looked at his watch. "It's really late. Why don't you two get some sleep? I'll stay here until your mother comes home."

"I want to wait up for Mom."

Again, Alex knew just how the little girl felt. "Your mom would want you to be in bed."

Nancy made a face, then giggled. Josh nodded. "Yeah, I guess you're right."

"Still kind of scared?"

"Uh-uh. Not now. Because you're here."

Alex stood up, so the children reluctantly did, too. "Come on. I'll tuck you in."

"I don't want to be all by myself," Nancy whispered. "Could we just all stay together?"

"Sure." Alex led them down the hall. "How about if I tuck you into your mother's bed so you can talk to her when she comes home? You'll know she's home because she'll have to move you out of the bed and get in herself."

They chuckled, but didn't complain.

Once inside the room, the three of them turned down the comforter, Nancy climbed into bed and snuggled under the covers.

"Alex?"

"What, sweetheart?"

"What happened to your car?"

Alex shrugged. "Well, I don't think I'll be driving it anymore. It's gone to that great junkyard in the sky."

Josh, busy climbing into the other side of the bed, gasped. "You mean the Ferrari is *totaled*?"

"Totaled." Compared to Wolf's life, losing a car didn't seem important at all.

"Don't worry, Alex," Josh whispered in the darkness. "You'll get another one."

"That's right, Josh. A car can be replaced," he told them. "Wolf and Becky can't."

"Here," Nancy said, sympathy in her voice. "You get the middle."

Alex lay down on top of the comforter, a child on either side. He'd come here to comfort the kids, and they'd turned around and comforted him instead. After all, that was what being a family was all about.

"Mom."

Olivia stepped closer to Wolf, who had been told to lie still for a few more minutes. "What, honey?"

"Can we go home?"

"I don't know." She took his hand. The long fingers were covered in dried blood, so Olivia looked around the curtained cubicle for a washcloth. There wasn't anything she could use. "How are you feeling?"

"My head hurts, but not bad."

"The doctor said you're going to have a pretty stiff neck tomorrow."

"Yeah. I believe it." He winced as he tried to move. "I just want to get out of here. This place is giving me the creeps."

"I'll go see if I can find the doctor again. It sounds pretty busy out there, doesn't it?"

"Yeah. Everyone's been really nice to me."

Olivia patted her son's hand and moved away. "I'm going to get something to clean you up with." She opened the curtain and stepped into the main area. It was busier than when she'd arrived, and the nurse was no longer at her station behind the counter. Someone moaned behind one of the curtains, and soft crying could be heard from another cubicle.

She knew she had to tell Alex what was going on. She'd left him alone for half an hour or more, and the man must be worried to death. She went into the waiting room and looked around, but he wasn't there. She waited for about ten minutes, idly leafing through an issue of *Time* magazine, in case he'd gone to the men's room.

He wouldn't have left the hospital. Why would he have left? Her son, his car. Two good reasons to stick around.

His car. The beloved Ferrari would most likely never be the same. At least, thank God, Wolf would.

She remembered the anguish on Alex's face, his pained expression and pale skin. He'd left. Bailed out when the going got rough, obviously. She should never have gotten her hopes up so high, never have grown used to having Alex around, bringing food, laughter and love.

She searched for another explanation. Maybe the policeman had told him to get the car, but Alex would surely have told her he had to leave. She'd seen him with the kids, seen the way they'd all grown accustomed to one another.

She shouldn't have trusted him to stay when the going got rough. Jack hadn't, and he'd been in on the conception. She should never have let herself depend on Alex, the Super Playboy himself. She should never have shared the responsibility of the children's welfare with a freewheeling, sports-car-driving marketing whiz. He'd acted strangely all evening. Maybe this was what he had planned all along—the grand goodbye scene with music, a blazing fire and a special meal. He'd acted oddly, as if he'd been trying to tell her something. Uncharacteristically nervous, too.

Well, these farewell scenes were probably really hard on a guy.

He'd saved himself the trouble by simply standing up and walking out, into the night.

Tears welled into her eyes, but Olivia blinked them away. She looked around the waiting room at the other people sitting forlornly in their chairs, waiting and hoping and most likely praying. If she was going to be much later, she'd have to call Polly and ask her to stay with Josh and Nancy. Hopefully the kids were asleep and wouldn't know anything was wrong. They loved to curl up in front of the television and fall asleep to movies.

She couldn't let Wolf see her cry, so she wiped her eyes and stood, replacing the magazine on the table nearby before returning to him.

"CAREFUL." She put an arm around Wolf's waist to guide him into the house. At least Alex had left the car keys when he'd made his getaway.

"I'm okay, Mom. Really."

She ushered him inside and noticed that the television was off. Josh and Nancy must have gone to bed, although they'd left pillows and blankets piled on the couch. Thank God, they'd gotten through the evening without knowing what had happened. She'd let Wolf tell them all about it in the morning.

"Sleep on the couch tonight," she ordered. "I don't want you alone upstairs."

"Okay. I'm just glad they let me out of that place."

"Me, too." The fresh air had lifted her spirits. She'd be fine without Alex. She'd been fine before and would do it again. Being alone was familiar. Safe.

And lonely.

"Where's Alex?"

"He had to leave," she fibbed. "Lie down on the couch and I'll cover you up."

"I have to tell him about the car, have to explain."

"The police told him, honey."

"Yeah, but I need to—"

"No," Olivia protested. "You need to rest. Is your neck comfortable?"

He wriggled the pillow behind him. "Yeah. Pretty good."

"Good." Olivia wanted to sit beside him all night, but knew he wouldn't let her. She'd sneak back throughout the night, though, and make sure he was breathing properly. The doctor had also recommended she wake him up every few hours, just in case he'd suffered a concussion. "Get some rest."

"You're sure Becky is all right? You're not keeping anything from me, are you?"

Olivia smoothed the hair off Wolf's forehead. "I don't lie. From what the nurse said, Becky is fine."

He closed his eyes. "Thanks, Mom," he murmured.

"Go to sleep."

Olivia stood up and switched off the lights, leaving one on in the kitchen to light the way down the hall, in case Wolf had to get up in the night. She'd put on her nightgown, then check on the younger children.

At first she thought they had decided to sleep in her bed. When she came closer, she saw Alex open his eyes.

Alex heard a soft gasp and blinked. He started to sit up, but his left arm was pinned down by Nancy's head. He didn't want to move the child and run the risk of waking her, now that she'd finally fallen asleep. "Olivia?" he whispered.

"Alex?"

"Shh," he ordered. "You'll wake up the kids."

She stepped up to the bed and peered at him through the darkness. "What are you doing here?"

"What do you mean?"

"What are you doing? You left."

"I left to check on the kids. I knew they'd be worried...."

"Why?" She frowned at him. "Why would they be worried? They didn't know anything about the accident."

He frowned back. "When the police called, they told me they got your number from Josh. When I had a chance to think—when you went back to see Wolf—I realized these kids must be worried sick."

"That's why you left?"

"Of course." He eased his arm free of Nancy's neck, then sat up. Still trapped between the two children, he debated whether to inch down to the end of the bed or to climb over Josh's inert body.

"Climb over," Olivia said, apparently reading his mind.

He did so as Olivia backed into the hall. He followed and soon stood before her, looking into a pair of very tired blue eyes. He wanted to grab Olivia's shoulders and shake her. She'd thought he'd left her. He could see it written all over her face. "For God's sake, Olivia. You thought I'd left you, didn't you?"

"You weren't there," she managed to say. "I went out to the waiting room and you weren't there and I thought—"

"So you just *assumed* I'd walked out of your life. Is that how little you think of me?" He was very, very angry.

"No, I—"

"I told the nurse in the emergency room to tell you where I'd gone."

"There must have been another accident. All the nurses were busy and—"

"You thought the worst."

"There didn't seem to be anything else to think, except—"

"Except that I'd walked out into the night, too much of a louse to support you when you needed me the most. Is that it?"

"Quit interrupting me."

"All right."

Olivia finally spoke into the silence. "That's it. That's exactly what I thought. Especially after tonight, when you acted so strangely and—"

"Do you want to know why I acted that way?"

"You interrupted me again." The pain in her heart began to dissolve and she took a deep breath. Alex was here, standing right before her. He hadn't gone anywhere at all, hadn't left her alone to pick up the pieces and carry on all by herself.

"I don't care if I interrupt you a hundred times. I planned a romantic evening for the two of us."

"And my kids got in the way."

"I'm used to it," he snapped. "But tonight was supposed to be special."

Olivia attempted a smile. "I noticed."

His frown didn't lighten. "Don't you want to know why, or are you too busy planning your life alone?"

She shook her head. "I want to hear every word."

The tightness around his mouth softened; his grip on her shoulders changed to a caress as he ran his hands down her arms and back to her neck. "I planned to ask you to marry me."

Olivia was stunned into silence.

"Well?" he urged. "Aren't you going to say something?" She opened her mouth and closed it again. "I take it that's a no."

"I don't know," she whispered. "You've never even said you loved me."

Alex winced. "You noticed that, huh?"

Olivia nodded. "I didn't expect you to say it," she assured him.

"I should have." He pulled her close. "I love you, Olivia, with all my heart. Will you marry me?" When she hesitated, he frowned once more. "I'm not like your husband, Olivia. I'm not going to leave—ever. If you think you'd be happy living the rest of your life alone, then so be it. You can have your way." His hands tightened around her waist. "I'm not going to ask you again."

Olivia looked into his gorgeous brown eyes. Happiness and relief filled her to the point where she couldn't speak, couldn't say the words Alex needed to hear.

Josh, sleepy and disheveled, appeared in the bedroom doorway, Nancy beside him. "Could we vote on that?" he asked.

"No." Olivia laughed. "Go back to bed."

Josh and Nancy staggered to their rooms while Olivia and Alex watched. When the hall was silent again, Alex turned back to the woman who stood beside him.

"You haven't said yes," he growled.

"I haven't said no, either." She smiled at him, looping her arms around his neck. "Would you like to have a meeting about this in my bedroom?"

"Now?" It was his turn to smile.

"I think now would be perfect," she murmured, standing on tiptoe to brush her lips against his.

"This is a secret meeting, then?" He followed Olivia into the dark room. "No board of directors?"

"Absolutely not," Olivia agreed, locking the door behind her. She stepped close to Alex and began to unbutton his shirt, but he stopped her with one strong hand.

"I want an answer to my question. Now."

Olivia smiled at him again. "If I say yes, will you spend the night?"

Alex lifted her into his arms and carried her to the waiting bed. "Tonight and every night for the rest of our lives, sweetheart." He flashed the famous Leeds grin. "After that, it's business as usual."

HARLEQUIN®

Temptation®

the Fortune Boys

A funny, sexy miniseries from bestselling
author Elise Title!

**LOSING THEIR HEARTS MEANT
LOSING THEIR FORTUNES....**

If any of the four Fortune brothers were unfortunate enough to
wed, they'd be permanently divorced from the Fortune
millions—thanks to their father's last will and testament.

BUT CUPID HAD OTHER PLANS!
Meet Adam in #412 **ADAM & EVE** (Sept. 1992)
Meet Peter #416 **FOR THE LOVE OF PETE**
(Oct. 1992)
Meet Truman in #420 **TRUE LOVE** (Nov. 1992)
Meet Taylor in #424 **TAYLOR MADE** (Dec. 1992)

**WATCH THESE FOUR MEN TRY TO WIN
AT LOVE AND NOT FORFEIT $$$**
